LOOKING GLASS LIVES

LOOKING GLASS LIVES

A Novel by

FELICE PICANO

Illustrated by
F. Ronald Fowler

alyson
books

LOS ANGELES • NEW YORK

MANUFACTURED IN THE UNITED STATES OF AMERICA.
PRINTED ON ACID–FREE PAPER.

THIS TRADE PAPERBACK ORIGINAL IS PUBLISHED BY ALYSON PUBLICATIONS INC., P.O. BOX 4371, LOS ANGELES, CALIFORNIA 90078-4371. DISTRIBUTION IN THE UNITED KINGDOM BY TURNAROUND PUBLISHER SERVICES LTD., UNIT 3 OLYMPIA TRADING ESTATE, COBURG ROAD, WOOD GREEN, LONDON N22 6TZ ENGLAND.

FIRST EDITION: SEPTEMBER 1998

02 01 00 99 98   10 9 8 7 6 5 4 3 2 1

ISBN 1-55583-481-7

LIBRARY OF CONGRESS CATALOGING–IN–PUBLICATION DATA
PICANO, FELICE.
   LOOKING GLASS LIVES : A NOVEL / BY FELICE PICANO.—1ST ED.
   I. TITLE.
   PS3566.I25L66 1998
   813'.54—DC21   98-21812 CIP

COVER DESIGN BY B. ZINDA

TO WILL MEYERHOFER

A CONSTANT READER

AND A FRIEND IN GOOD TIMES AND BAD TIMES

STRANGE THAT LOVE SHOULD BE CARVED IN MIST
AND DEATH, WITH A SLOW HAND, CARVED IN STONE.

FROM "TWELVE GOOD MEN" BY CONRAD AIKEN

PROLOGUE

The well is repaired. Amity Pritchard's well. My well.

Two men came this morning from Scituate to repair it. No one from this town would come, even though Burt Wayland promised to do it months ago. I wasn't surprised he never showed up.

No one from Nansquett will ever come onto this property again. At least, not while I'm alive. Probably not after I'm dead either. The last time I ordered from Millicent's by telephone, the delivery boy left my order way down at the entrance to the road, off Atwood Avenue. He wouldn't dare step foot on the property. If I hadn't been wandering down at that end, I would never have seen the three wild cats—thrown out of houses in town—trying to get into the loosely closed cardboard boxes he'd left there.

At the end of the property; just as in Amity's time. How the circle is closing in on her and me, making us one. I'm often down there, all around the property now that the weather is milder, trying to come closer to her, trying to bring us even more together. How little remains to keep us from being the same entity! Very little now. Especially since Amity's well has been repaired and is ready to be used again. The last act of the drama ready to be repeated. Closing in. Like a snake biting its own tail—that Gnostic sign of infinity, that abolition of time and space, as Reverend Pritchard understood so well, that containment of all there is. And soon the two spirals of our lives will be joined, and we will be one: I, Roger Lynch, and she, Amity Pritchard—two no more.

All this has taken a long time to understand.

The affinity between us has been present a long time—more than half my life, since that summer years ago with Grandpa and Chas. Especially with Chas. He too had a role. As did my wife, Karen. And Amity. And her sister, Constance. And Captain Eugene V. Calder of the Union Army. All of us—Chas, Karen, and I—in it for years before we even suspected. I think only I ever really knew for certain. Did Chas? Even if only in that split second when so much is supposed to be made clear, before his life was smashed out of him? Karen should have known then. That afternoon before they left me, I as much as told her we were living in the grip of the past, not only our own past but something that didn't really concern us, something that could be al-tered. Did she understand me? I thought she did. The way she looked at me, so sadly, her intelligent agate eyes roving around the breakfast room as they tended to do whenever she understood and wished not to. But no. She would never have left me if she had understood what was going to happen to her and Chas. Or would she? So in love with him—despite him, despite herself...so in the grip of this thing we were all in, that time no longer mattered. The past and present and future were always fairly inconsequential in Karen anyway. That's what I loved about her first—how out of time she seemed.

They were never important at all to Chas. So little was important to him. Which was what I loved about him: his ability to enter into fantasies so quickly, so intensely, they became more important than reality. How, fifteen years later he came by, just as Karen and I had moved here, into the old Pritchard house we'd bought to restore, and how he just started in again, as though no time at all had intervened between my going and our coming back. As if back then, that summer I came to Nansquett for the first time, first came to feel Chas's power—and Amity's, always Amity's too—had never ended. As though it were not merely a dress rehearsal as I came to think of it, but one continuous chunk of action, despite the length of years that had to pass before it could all be played out. As I have only recently come to understand that this—my coming time—is to be the continuation of a time even earlier than fifteen years ago: of Amity's own time and Constance's and Captain Calder's. And the act that is to be repeated, will be repeated as though it had not occurred once already. That's why I had to have the well repaired. It alone needed to be mended. Only the well could possibly set the scene for the final act of the drama. Amity's drama. Mine, now.

The men who came from Scituate to repair the well knew a great deal more than they let on. Standing in the foyer, burly and indifferent in their work clothes, one of them said they had stopped in Etty's dinette for breakfast before coming here. Blurted it out, really. That was said so they wouldn't have to accept my offer of breakfast, of coffee even, so they wouldn't have to come any further into the house. The other one—the darker, heavier one—nudged the first when he said that about stopping in the dinette, as though I weren't supposed to know about it. They just had a job to do, was his opinion: his firm, dense typically-closed-into-life-as-I-am-closed-into-death New England opinion. He didn't want to know any more than that. I could tell. How he stood in the foyer, peering about as though he expected bats or ghouls or I don't know what to fly down out of the ornate ceiling molding, as though he expected the stained glass skylight above us to suddenly shatter, sending shards of glass to impale him.

Of course they must have known something about me—even about Amity—by the time they drove up to the house. Etty would have seen they were strangers and asked what they were doing, coming over from Scituate. It's rare enough that she sees strangers here in the autumn. In summer, of course, it's different, what with all the summer residents and their visitors.

Oh, the Pritchard place, she would have remarked, when the men told her where they were going, she speaking casually, yet not hiding her surprise. He's re-pairing the well, she would have asked, in the fall? I thought people fixed wells only in springtime. But that Mr. Lynch wouldn't know any better, would he? He isn't like other folks here in Nansquett. A stranger here, really. Only moved here two years ago, although his family always had a summer home here, for over a cen-tury. On the other side of the river. Old Ralph Lynch built it. Guess you've heard of him, even in Scituate. Big man in the county a dozen years ago, even up at the statehouse for years, right through the Depression. Built that big house there in the 'teens. I was just a lit-tle girl then. You can see it if you turn around. There, that one, with the dozen dark painted gables and the big porch wrapping three quarters around the bottom floor. In summer you can only make out the third floor windows, because of all the foliage. No, that's not where Mr. Roger Lynch lives. He's farther up, off Atwood Avenue. Didn't he give you directions? No, the old Lynch house has been turned into a summer hotel for people down from Providence. Filled up every summer now that rents have gone so sky-high on those boxy little cottages around the river they call villas. Villas, my eye! No, sir, the current Mr. Lynch lives up at the Pritchard place. Bought it and restored it to look as it did over a hundred years ago. Bought it, lived in it, and scandalized the town from it in less than eighteen months. Not really a stranger to Nansquett though. His mother would bring him and the little girl up to visit the grandfather once a year. Why, I believe he even spent a summer here, when he was a boy. So, he isn't really a stranger. I recall him coming in here for a sandwich and a soda. With his cousin, Chas Lynch. You know Chas Lynch, don't you? A shame about him. Mr. Roger Lynch always did seem to have one foot in this town and the other somewhere else, in New York, I suppose.

How much more did Etty tell the men from Scituate? Filling up their coffee cups as she spoke, so they wouldn't notice the time passing, even cutting a jelly doughnut in half and putting it on their plates (without charge)—a small sacrifice just for the thrill of telling someone new what she and everyone else in Nansquett haven't gotten sick of gossiping about yet. The only real gossip they've had for a hundred years, I'm sure. Since Amity's time. That's the way it is in these small, hidden-away New England coastal towns: towns located off the new highways that connect cities, towns without sub-urbs. If you fart in Nansquett, Grandpa Lynch used to say, everyone knows within the hour; and furthermore, everyone knows whether it stunk or not.

Not that Grandpa ever cared. He'd grown up here and moved away to Providence. After he sold his news-paper, he came and lived here for years and loved the town. Taught me to love it too. Mother never cared for it, though she'd been here for years. It was what she'd escaped from when she moved down to New York to work at the World's Fair in '39, displaying the first tele-vision sets in the General Electric Home of the Future. All Mother wanted was to get away from Nansquett and to stay away. To meet Father and remain in New York. And that's what she did, until Janet and I were old enough to travel easily, and Grandpa was getting so old he began to want her company. So she would pack us into the big new Plymouth station wagon and drive up on holiday weekends. The station wagon was a dream, with wooden side panels inside and out and a third seat facing the rear of the road, which Janet and I would take turns sitting in, watching the other cars be-hind us—a seat that folded flat for storage. No, Mother never much liked it here, even though she was good about coming up to see her father. She would drive over to Point Judith where a few of her old friends had married and moved to, and she would spend afternoons with them, playing canasta or bridge with them and the other wives of the Coast Guard officers who would drive over the state line from Groton.

I sometimes think Mother only came up to Nansquett to show off to the townspeople. To show off her Town and Country station wagon—a new model every year. To show off her New York clothes and New York manners and New York husband and children. Also to show off by going away again with great fanfare. She never loved the town the way I came to. I don't think Karen did either—crazy as she was about the house we restored and lived in. I sometimes think Karen remained here only because of me and later because of Chas.

Chas. I'll never really know what he thought of Nansquett, even though he alone of all of us lived here all his life. He must have cared for the quiet and hot blooming smell of the town in summer, the patterns of branches and bushes shadowing the streets. Yet how eager he was to get away, as soon as Karen wanted him to. Not that they ever got too far, not even outside the town limits: just as far as the highway entrance off Atwood Avenue.

Did Etty tell the men from Scituate all that? She

might have. What difference does it make? They came here anyway, even after she chewed off their ears about us. They had a job to do, as the heavier one—the frightened one—said, and they did it. Stopped only once to have lunch, eating in their car down below the terrace, outside the garage that once had been stables. Looking out of their front windshield at the bleak November day, they would have had a good view of the Pritchard place: leaves turning, dying, everywhere, for thousands of square yards around them, the silence of the woods, the gray light sharpening every twig of tree, every architectural detail of the house—Amity's house, my house—restored to look exactly as it did in 1865.

From the second-floor sitting room, I watched the men eating in their car. Sipping tea from my lovely old china (found in the cellar, along with so many other beautiful old things), I could see them clear the decades of debris out of the well, then drop down a rope ladder and shimmy down it into the well shaft. I saw them repair the broken sections of the wall at the bottom of the well, almost twenty feet down, then install new plumbing; and I saw them come up again and put in new side drains here at the ground level so the well wouldn't overflow after storms. They did an excellent job, a professional job. Hardly speaking to each other, except to call out "Here!" or "Push now!" or "Harder!" or "Give me that." Silent men. Like most of the men around here. Like Grandpa used to be, fishing. Silent. Until they have something to say or until they feel comfortable, when they begin to talk and will go on for hours.

I wonder if Etty told the men from Scituate about me and Chas? That's probably why they wouldn't come any farther into house beyond the foyer, why they wouldn't even come in to use the lavatory, pissing behind the garage like dogs, like wild animals. No. She couldn't have told them. No one in Nansquett could know that about Chas and I. Or did everyone know, all the time? What difference does it make? They repaired the well. Soon the circle will close in completely.

As the men worked, wet leaves from around the well stuck to their boots and trousers, right up to their thighs, as though determined to decorate the dull gray corduroy the color of this November day with patches of shiny yellows and deep reds and orange-browns. Looking like the pants kids used to wear in the '60s—colored patches on old denims. Comic and unaware, the two silent men worked on, their decorated trousers looking wonderful. Until they finished repairing the well, looked down and saw the leaves and brushed them off roughly. When they came to the foyer again to get paid, the leaves were gone, but the spots from where they had festooned the men's legs and thighs were still damp, as though shadows of colors still remained.

Even so does the past mark us, fleeting as the dampness of a fallen leaf, yet strong enough to be felt. Or deep as a well. Amity's well. My well now—and my future.

I do not fight this future anymore. Not since Chas and Karen left or tried to leave and discovered too late that leaving was a very particular action in the play they had allowed themselves to become enmeshed in.

I am reconciled now. I accept. I submit. I am even eager to embrace the future—and the past. Amity's life becoming my life, finally; Amity's story, my story. More so than I could have dreamed possible fifteen years ago, when I first heard of Amity Pritchard.

1

It was the year Mother's Chinese baby died.

Of course, it wasn't really Chinese, much as it looked it. But that's what Janet, my younger sister, nine years old and sassy, called it. What it really was, was a Mongoloid baby—or would have been, if it hadn't turned bluish and died all of a sudden one afternoon a month after it and Mother had come home from the hospital. Mother tried to breathe life back into it, holding the baby across her arms, crying and rocking and blowing air into its mouth—gaped open like a caught fish—all at the same time. She wouldn't believe it was dead. Wouldn't even put it back into its crib, until Grandma came and made her, leading Mother upstairs then, and coming down to take me and Janet across the street to her house, where we had sweetened frothy Viennese coffee and cookies.

She wasn't really our Grandma, of course, just our

Hungarian neighbor lady from across the street. But she was old enough to be a grandmother, and as our grandmothers were both dead—and even when they had been alive had never been as near to us, as interested, as good to us as she was—we called her Grandma. I had run to get her when I saw the baby turning blue and Mother crying, knowing something was wrong. Afterward Grandma said what a smart and grown-up boy I was for only twelve, doing that. She let me leaf through all her husband's old copies of *Esquire,* I suppose because I was now so grown-up.

Mother stayed in her bedroom for almost a week. But that didn't seem to make her any happier about losing the Chinese baby. She wouldn't go to the funeral with Janet and Father and me—all dressed up, even though it was a rainy Thursday afternoon, following the big-backed Caddy containing the little coffin from the funeral home. Neither Janet nor I had ever been to a funeral before, even though this wasn't a real funeral—we were the only people there, with no churchman or anything because the baby hadn't even been old enough to be baptized. Still, we were both quiet, taking our cue from Father, who was very sad.

When Mother recovered enough to get out of bed, she wanted us to move away from the house so she wouldn't always have to pass the spot where the Chinese baby had turned blue and died in her arms.

Father said we couldn't move right away. But he did say we could go stay with Grandpa—our real Grandpa, Grandpa Lynch, Mother's father, up in Nansquett. Mother didn't really care for this, but I guess she finally gave in, because all of a sudden we were set to go, the day that our school term finished. There was just barely enough time for me and Janet to get home from school, to change our clothes into jeans and T-shirts, to bring down the suitcases and cardboard boxes—Mother had been packing all week—and stow them in the back of the station wagon. Then we were off.

It happened to Janet and me so quickly that we were a hundred miles away from our home, sitting on plank-wood benches at a plank-wood picnic table on the shoulder of the Merritt Parkway, eating egg-salad sandwiches and watching the sun begin its slow summer setting through a strand of tall trees, before we realized this was going to be a different kind of summer than any we'd had before.

Mother did a lot of remembering in that half hour or so of picnic. She told us how she had first gone to Grandpa Lynch's summer house when she was nine years old—the same age as Janet—for their first summer by the shore and every summer thereafter until she'd met and married Father and come to stay in New York. She'd had her first sweetheart in Nansquett too—a boy everyone called Sourpuss because he frowned so much—when she was my age, twelve.

She kept on remembering when we got back into the car to take off again. She enjoyed driving the station wagon, full as it was, and despite her always seeming worried as she asked one of us to look back and make sure there were no cars in back of us while she changed lanes, as we swooped up and then down the highway, like a bug riding along the inside of a ribbon unfurling in the wind.

Janet and I were so happy to see Mother happy for the first time in over a month that we didn't give a thought to all of our friends we'd left behind and wouldn't see for months. We were eager to believe Mother when she told us what a good time we'd all have in Nansquett. Grandpa's house was big enough so we'd each have not only a bedroom, but also a sitting room to ourselves. There was a river right behind the house where we could fish and swim every day, and the shore out in front. Grandpa would take us to his favorite places in the woods nearby. And if we asked him, our cousin Chas would show us the best places for going quahogging, clamming, and crabbing along the tide pools of the shoreline. Surely we remembered our cousin Chas and his little sister, Cathy? Surely I was old enough to remember Grandpa Lynch's house, Mother asked.

I had been to Nansquett once before, for a weekend

I think, but of course I really had been too young to recall it. I did remember Grandpa—a tall old figure
smelling of tobacco and looking like a waxed yellow
scarecrow with his bald head that shone in strong
lamplight, and his huge yellowing mustachio. But that
was because he'd come to New York to visit us on the
Christmas holidays.

If both Janet and I looked forward to seeing Grandpa Lynch again—each of us loving him as much for how
odd and old he looked to us, as for remembered kind-
nesses he'd rendered us—both of us were a great deal
more doubtful about our cousins Chas and Cathy
Lynch. I had thought about Chas a little in the week
before we'd left home, but that was because I could
look at a photograph of him in Mother's bedroom,
starchily standing—small and blond—between Aunt
Linda and Uncle Al. He'd only been seven when that
photo was taken, and would be thirteen or fourteen by
now. And from the way Mother always talked about
Chas—her favorite nephew, she remarked every time
his name came up, although why, she wouldn't say—he
seemed a formidable companion, one I doubted I
would have much to do with.

Not that Chas had ever been brought up as an example for me to follow. No, he was a bold enough, even
an impudent child, from all the stories I heard of him,
active and always getting into something new. But he

had his problems—fights, delinquency even—two years before—running away from home for two days. That made Chas almost bad—although not quite, because Mother said he was still the most mannerly and helpful little boy she knew and still her favorite nephew. All I could think of was all Chas had done to outstrip me. He fished, he hunted, he'd water-skied, he could drive a car. Too much competition for me, whose one real outdoor sport was bicycling and who preferred sitting in a hammock and reading to anything more strenuous.

I don't think Janet met her age mate, Cathy, with any such trepidation. Once we'd arrived in Nansquett, they met, played together, joined other girls their own age, had spats, made up, bought and made a constant stream of gifts for each other, and finally parted at the summer's end with much crying and promises they never kept to write each other every week.

Maybe girls have it easier than boys do. All I know is, nothing that simple happened to Chas and me. And, having the girls—and soon after, even our parents—otherwise occupied, we were thrown together a great deal more than we expected, even going so far as to having to share a bedroom—a situation that had to intensify what already seemed a relationship with many built-in tensions.

But all that wouldn't happen right away, wouldn't happen until after Mother and Janet and I had settled into Grandpa Lynch's big house. For a few weeks we would have its many barely furnished rooms and huge expanses to ourselves to enjoy. I took a bedroom at the end of the second floor, with an attached room that opened up to Janet's bedroom. I found exactly the lounge chair I liked for reading, on the shore side of the three-quarter wrap-around first-floor veranda. After dinner, but before the late summer sunset, Mother took Janet and I walking along the shore to see the ocean, and to remark on how big the property was, there being no house on either side of Grandpa Lynch's for a half football field's length. The weathered clapboard siding glittered dully in the sinking daylight as gleams off the chipped places in the gutter and side trim made the gray and white wood look brown and pink—like a big sandcastle someone had built with a ruler and plane. Janet would count the house's windows—eight on each side of the bottom floor, four dormers on each side upstairs—and then each one of us would pick out the windows to our rooms, with pride and pleasure.

Going back to the house, we walked up through another property to Atwood Avenue and strolled down that street, covered over surprisingly with huge old houses like Grandpa's but dark now in the twilight, shut out by the enormous walnut and oak trees that lined the road. Janet said she was afraid each time, even though Mother always laughed at her. I laughed at her too, but it did feel eerie to me, walking along that road and not hearing the sound of traffic, but all the subdued noises of the country instead of the city—surf, crickets, the wind swooshing through the foliage.

Before going to bed, we would stay out on the veranda and in the failing light play Parcheesi or Chinese checkers or just listen to the radio from Providence, which still had talk shows like Hopalong Cassidy and the Mystery Theater, which we never heard in New York because we had television already. Then, each night before going to sleep, Mother would take us to the end of the second floor, up the five wooden steps to Grandpa's cluttered little study where he sat up late reading the Bible and smoking his pipe, sitting up straight in the old Captain's chair, looking thoughtful, immersed in the words of the text open in front of him—until he would hear us and turn to lift us up and let us kiss him good night. It was then that he smelled strongest of old wool cloth and pipe mixture. His hard long bristles of waxed mustachio would scrape my cheeks not unpleasantly. And I would try to count the wrinkles on his neck behind the starched high white collars he wore even in the hottest weather. His smell was always a sour-sweet mixture of the pipe mixture and the violet candies he constantly chewed now that his gums were going bad, a mixed odor that would always make me—already exhausted—dizzy with anticipation and fear of growing up.

It was Grandpa Lynch who first told me of Amity Pritchard—really told me, didn't merely make a story out of her life to scare me away from the Pritchard property. And so, I suppose, he too figured importantly in the linking up, although exactly where I'm still not certain.

But that wouldn't happen in the small step-up study, nor until much later, in August. And Grandpa wouldn't be telling just me either but my cousin Chas too, who was to be involved in it as deeply as I, even if he never admitted it or even really recognized his involvement.

And before Amity's story could make any sense to me, I still had to meet Chas.

2

"Any fish that's dumb enough to be caught with a line like this ain't worth the work."

I looked up from the fishing line I was disentangling for the third time that afternoon. Standing between me—out on the grass bank of the little river that ran behind Grandpa Lynch's house and the water itself—was a boy who, from the way he looked and held himself and suddenly, quietly appeared, might have come up from the bottom of the riverbed itself or from some thicket or cave across the water, deep in the gloomy woods facing me, he so much fit into the place.

Without knowing for certain, I knew this was my cousin Chas.

"You'll be there all afternoon, doing it that way," he said in his mischievous but surprisingly grown-up voice.

He was right, of course. Following a storm the night

before, the calm little rivulet had become a swollen, high-banked torrent, its current so strong, my line would double and even triple back on itself every time I cast it. Three or four knots were made instantly, except for the lure and hook, which I couldn't seem to knot tight enough to hold, and which fell off and had to be replaced with every throw.

"Here," he said, holding out his hand. "Give me!"

Without my offering the line, he bent down and drew the line out of the water. He barely inspected it. Holding it in his teeth, he expertly removed each knot in seconds. This gave me a chance to look at him more closely.

He couldn't have been more than a year or two older than me—but he looked a whole lot more grown-up. His shoulders were high and wide, his legs long and muscled, his waist slim, his entire frame of flesh defined from either exercise or sport. Not an inch of baby fat, whereas I was covered with it. As he was wearing only a pair of dungarees, I could see he even had a hair or two bravely sticking out in the flat depression between his chest muscles. He was a deep tan—almost brown—tanner by far than I was, although I'd been out in the sun almost every day for the past two weeks. And this brownness contrasted with his curly sandy-colored hair, with flecks of yellow and streaks that were almost pure white. He wore his hair much longer than anyone else I'd ever seen—and it seemed to draw even more attention to his deeply tanned, surprisingly mannish face. Surprising because feature by feature, it was almost a girlishly pretty face. Even odder, despite his coloring and because of his hair color, you expected to see light eyes—blue or green or even gray—but his weren't light at all. They were so brown as to seem black, and all the more prominent because they were so large, even with him squinting against the strong sunlight, and so deep-set. He was, of course, the same little boy I'd seen in the family photo on my mother's dresser. But that boy was a baby, compared to the little man squatting in front of me.

"Jesus H. Christ!" he said, and I was struck all over again by the New England accent with its strange shifts of vowel emphasis, its drawn-out syllables, and flattened consonants that made even the smallest child sound like an old person. "What a mess you've made of this line," he added with disgust. But all the knots were out of the line already. "Here, you can't knot a hook the way you hook a rug," he said. "Look here. This is the way you knot a hook. It's a sailor's knot. See! First you loop it, then you pull the line through halfway and tighten it with another loop in the other direction. That way you can unknot it just by giving it a tug. See! Just tug it off when the hook is caught in a fish's mouth. Now you try it."

He stood up and threw the line into my lap.

"Go on. Try it."

"Like this?" I asked. I unknotted it easily enough, but I couldn't remember the instructions to put it together again.

"No. First this way, *then* hold it, and do it in the other direction."

I repeated his instructions out loud as I tried to follow them. "First from this way. Then hold it. Then from that...ow! That rotten hook!"

He grabbed my hand to look at the cut in my index finger.

"It's nothing," he said, with disgust.

"It hurts. It's bleeding."

He held on to it even harder, squeezing the little cut until a globule of blood welled to the surface, followed by another one, so red and liquid that my eyes hurt to look at them. Then he quickly bent down and swallowed my finger. When he looked up at me, I felt afraid and pulled my hand out.

"Mmm," he said.

"Let go!"

"Mmm" he said again and finally took my finger out of his mouth, inspecting the cut. "There. That will keep you from dying of tetanus."

"I'll go get a Band-Aid," I said, trying to withdraw my hand from his grasp. But he continued to grip it and squeeze it, making more drops of blood rise to the surface and break and fall into my open palm, before he swooped down again with open mouth and licked the blood.

"You don't need a Band-Aid now. It's all right now."

I took out a handkerchief, which while rolled up was pretty clean, and wrapped my finger in that.

He sat down in the grass next to me and stared at me until I began to feel even more frightened than when he had my finger in his mouth and wouldn't let go.

"What's your name?" he asked.

"Roger."

"I thought that's who you were. I'm Chas."

"I thought that's who you were."

He laughed. "Oh, yeah! Well, then you're not as dumb as you look."

I didn't like that remark and so turned back to my fishing line, trying to knot the hook on again as he had told me to.

"What's the matter?" he asked. "Don't you like being called dumb?" Without waiting for my reply, he went on. "I'll bet you didn't know that now that I've sucked your blood to keep you from dying, you're in bondage to me—forever."

"I wasn't going to die."

"Yes, you would have. From tetanus."

"That hook isn't rusty. It's brand-new."

"That doesn't mean anything. Hooks don't have to be rusty to have germs on them. You can't see germs, stupid."

That at least I knew to be true. But I didn't like either his tone of voice or what else he was saying. "Well, I'm not in bondage to you. Or to anyone, just because you drank a little of my blood."

"You are too! And anyway, you probably don't even know what it means."

"I do too! It means being a slave to someone. I read about it. The Hebrews were in bondage to the Pharaoh of Egypt, until Moses came along."

"Well, so are you to me," he said, enjoying my discomfort.

"Phooey! I never heard that before."

"It's true," he said.

"No it isn't. When you drink someone's blood, it means that you swear friendship with them. Only both of you have to do it, or it doesn't work. That's the only thing about blood drinking I ever heard of."

He listened, then stretching his lips tight over his teeth, with his hands raised, fingers crooked out, he leaned over me until he'd forced me onto my back, shrinking from him.

"What about vampires!" he shouted. "Haven't you heard of vampires? How they come while you're sleeping and suck your blood while you're dreaming?"

I had heard of them, and I was clearly so terrified that he dropped his mask and laughed out loud.

"Don't worry, kid. I'm not a vampire. Boy, what a stupid kid you are. You'd believe anything."

I stood up. "I don't believe in vampires."

"Do you believe in ghosts?" he asked. He was watching me closely now.

"No. There's no such things as ghosts."

"Well, that's how dumb you are," he said noncommittally, lying back in the grass and looking up at the sky. "Because I saw one."

I ignored him and, gathering up my line, went away from him a few feet. I sat down there and cast my line in the river. I couldn't really concentrate on my fishing though. He was still too close to me, turned over on his stomach, leaning on his hands with his face turned toward me, looking at me with I don't know what intentions.

We were quiet like that for a long time. Then I reeled in the line.

"This place stinks for fishing," I said.

"I'll show you a really good place to fish," he said quietly. "Last week I caught a six-pound carp there."

"Where?"

"You're probably too scared to go."

"Where?"

"On the Pritchard property. In the broken old well

up on the terrace level. Same place where I saw the ghost."

"I'm not afraid of ghosts," I said.

"You sure are dumb. Everyone's afraid of ghosts. Especially when it's old Amity Pritchard's ghost. She's something! I'll bet I'm the only person—grown folks and *all*—to even go near that property, they're all so afraid of her ghost. Ask Grandpa Lynch. He'll tell you."

I said I would ask Grandpa Lynch and began gathering up my tackle to leave. He stayed on his stomach, looking at me.

"If you want," he said suddenly, his voice seeming to drop until it almost sounded like someone else's voice entirely, "I'll cut myself too, and then you can suck my blood too."

"No thanks."

"Boy! What a jerk you are. I already told you you're in bondage to me. This way you'll get out of it."

That seemed logical to me. But he scared and disturbed me. So I said, "No thanks. I don't want any life-long friends."

"Suit yourself, it's your loss," he said nonchalantly, then, rolling over, added, "If you're not going to use that line, leave it here. I'll try my hand with it."

"Make sure you get it back to the house," I said, throwing it down on the grass next to him and walking off.

He came into the house later that afternoon with three good-sized fish, though nothing like the six-pounder he had talked about. I was sitting in the big hammock on the veranda, half falling asleep with a book in my lap.

"You get them at the Pritchard property?" I asked.

"Nope. In the river. Exactly where you were sitting all day like a fool. Did you ask Grandpa Lynch about the ghost?"

"I'm not interested in any ghosts," I said, taking my book and opening it so I wouldn't have to look at him.

"Scaredy-cat!"

3

Chas and his sister Cathy had arrived at Grandpa
Lynch's house two weeks in advance of their parents,
who were still in Coventry preparing for their eventual
larger move to a partially built house a half mile away
from where we were staying for the summer. During
those two weeks of transition, Chas stayed in the extra
room on the second floor, although I was already told
that when his parents came, they would be moved in
there, and he would be sharing my room. Cathy and
Janet were already sharing their bedroom with ease,
and beginning the first tentative blush of their devel-
oping friendship.

In the meanwhile I saw Chas only at meals and
whenever he deliberately chose my company. I never
consciously sought his. Not only because of our first
encounter but also because he had dropped the fact
that he had not returned to Nansquett to play with

"kids" but to play with his friends from previous summers—especially the two Muller boys, more his age anyway, who lived up at the restored mill house.

I had enough to keep me occupied for a while, even though as July wore on I had already become a little sated with the beach and the few amusements it offered. I did discover the Nansquett Public Library one day, however, and so I could put aside the few books I had hurriedly packed, which, read and reread, had already become tedious to me.

That discovery happened one of the afternoons I was assigned to accompany my sister and cousin to the ice-cream stand on Twill Road, just past the Atwood Avenue crossing. It was near the little wooden bridge thrown up over the river, where the half-dozen stores that composed the town proper were located. Much as I was annoyed at having to hold the two squealing girls' hands at the one traffic light in the area, I looked forward to the lusciously creamy homemade ice cream we would get there, made daily with whatever fruit—peach, blueberry, strawberry—was in season. And also I looked forward to looking at the comic book rack above the small pile of local newspapers.

That afternoon the ice creams available were vanilla, chocolate, and raspberry. But the comic rack hadn't been changed in weeks, a fact I complained about to Eileen, the twelve-year-old fair-skinned, raven-haired

daughter of the ice-cream store owner, Bud Bianchi.
Eileen had made a point of being extra polite and cordial to me from the day I'd come to her store, and this
afternoon she not only told me about the public library, but she got her mother's permission to show me
the place, saying she had some books due to be returned there anyway. The younger girls were placed in
an adjoining kitchen with a picture puzzle to solve, and
Eileen and I walked the few blocks to the library.

I was used to our library back in the city—a modern,
glossily efficient series of low rooms with blond wood
Danish furniture, wood shelving that looked plastic,
and fluorescent lighting. So I was surprised by—and
later pleased with—the old two-story structure that
housed Nansquett's public books. Set in the back of the
small building that served as the town hall and justice
of the peace's office, the library consisted of one huge
room with heavy dark wood shelving eight feet high all
around, except for two walls, which were twenty feet
high and had a small balcony of books, approached by
a rickety-looking cast iron stairway, leading to a perfo-
rated cast iron walkway which gave access to the upstairs shelves.

In the center of the room were four large old oak tables, surrounded by deeply curved distressed-oak
chairs. Everything about the place—its great, sudden
height; its narrow small-paned windows beveled in

yellow glass around each edge; its general gloom of
aged wood and old bindings even on those days when
the sun came in with great flat patterns across the old
tables and readers; and especially the beautiful old
sets of books—impressed me so much that later on,
after a decade and a half, I would be drawn back to it
with renewed interest and affection. Only then, fifteen
years later, would I notice the beneficiary plaque set in
the wall above the librarians' desk, its unpolished
bronze showing the prominently placed name of the
library's founder, Amity Pritchard; the year 1873, written in Roman numerals; and under that the dedica-
tion: IN MEMORY OF MY DEARLY DEPARTED SISTER, CON-
STANCE, AND HER HUSBAND, CAPTAIN EUGENE V. CALDER
OF THE UNION ARMY.

When I was twelve I didn't see the plaque—or if I did,
it didn't register. At the time all I remarked upon was
the deliciously indiscriminate placement of adult and
children's books on the same shelves—although there
was one shelf of children's picture books, including
Anna May Seward, Alcott, and a "Great Lives for Boys"
series, all of which I scorned. It took only an hour to
find the books that would interest me, even obsess me
the remainder of the summer: battered old copies of
the works of H.G. Wells, Jules Verne, Le Fanu, Poe,
Wilkie Collins, and, most profusely, the appallingly
frightening works of the home state author H.P. Love-

craft.

Eileen turned her pretty nose up at these choices of reading matter but at nothing else about me. We soon found we could talk hours at a time about almost any other subject under the sun, in any place whatsoever— a situation that made Janet and Cathy whisper and giggle and squeal all the more. Naturally I ignored them, thinking only what a sensible girl Eileen was, how well-read, how much of a first friend for me that summer. Nor did it escape me that such a friendship brought with it large, free quantities of ice cream, and a consuming interest from her lovely melting eyes, eyes my mother once evaluated in conversation as a true and haunting amethyst color.

Chas, of course, sneered whenever he saw Eileen and me together. But Chas sneered at anything I did. At my reading, at my idling about on the rubber raft unadventurously tied to a stake on the beach, at my looks, at my voice, at my attitudes—in short, everything about me.

Not that it kept him away from me. Just the opposite. I would be walking somewhere, and he would just pop out of some bushes and follow me, making critical comments and telling me all the "terrific" things he and the Muller boys had done or were planning to soon do, none of which involved me. Or I would be out on the little dinghy in the river, and Chas would dive into the water, swim out to me, lift himself dripping into the boat, and dare me to go with him to the Pritchard property, or he would find me fishing quietly and challenge me to a foot race, or he'd find me half asleep in my hammock and rouse me to go play stick ball with the Muller boys.

I never said yes, and he never seemed to mind that I didn't. He always said that I was a jerk and would casually go off by himself, adding as a parting word, "Suit yourself."

Yet, little as I let on, Chas's words and taunts did have an effect on me. I was extra careful not to see Eileen two days running so I couldn't be accused of liking girls' company better than boys'. I did learn to swim across and back the little river, if only to prove to myself that I could. I looked at myself differently undressing at night, wondering if I would ever be as tan or muscular as Chas was, as grown-up–looking. I even used to stop on Atwood Avenue, off Cheyne Road, just before the highway turnoff, and stand awhile, looking to make sure I wasn't being watched, before taking a dozen or so steps down the wooded-over dirt road that Chas told me led to the Pritchard house, set back a hundred yards from the avenue and so overgrown that you couldn't even make out the masonry on the retaining walls alongside the path.

When one day Chas came back with a cut over one

eye from a fight with Rudy Muller—a fight he wouldn't explain—he stopped going up to the mill and hung around Grandpa Lynch's house, even more insistently in my way. He acted as if he hadn't anything better to do than to intently and curiously stare at me, following me from place to place, doing whatever I did or even doing nothing at all. Already feeling suspicious and slightly eerie by the books I'd been reading that summer, I found myself more and more disturbed by Chas's interest in me—so much so, at one point, that I decided I would rather go around with Grandpa.

It was easy enough to attach myself to Grandpa Lynch, and fun too, even though, old as he was, he seemed to take forever to do anything or go anywhere, and it was often a real chore to understand what he was saying, as he often spoke without his false teeth and usually so slowly, I'd forget what he'd just said and be unable to make sense out of single sentences, they took so long unfurling out of him. Still, he took me to places I'd never been: his favorite fishing spots upriver; into the next town, to Scituate, where he had many old-timer friends; for walks off the regular roads; up into the hills; to Indian burial grounds; and once even to Petaquamsquett Rock, where the Nansquett Indians had signed a treaty with some colonists, a treaty treacherously broken two years later when the settlers murdered the entire tribe one night by stealth. If I listened

hard enough and could manage the required patience,
I could learn everything from Grandpa Lynch, as he
seemed to know everything there was to know—histor-
ical, biblical, medicinal, mechanical, scientific, or politi-
cal. We soon became close companions, even though
his actions were subject to whims of age so arbitrary, I
never could understand them, and he would follow up
days of hiking and talking to me with days when he
held himself aloof from me, not even leaving his little
study for dinner, untouchable, unreachable to me except for my nightly kiss.

All that—like almost everything else in my life—
changed the night Uncle Al and Aunt Linda moved
into Grandpa Lynch's house, and Chas moved into my
bedroom.

4

"What do you do with Eileen?" Chas asked, half leaning out of his bed, just inches away from my head.

"Do? Nothing."

"You must do something. You're with her all day."

"Nothing. We talk."

It was a miserably hot night—and worse, it seemed, because the sun had beat down on the room all day, there was no comforting night breeze, and horseflies the size of Brazil nuts were buzzing thunderously on the screen windows, trying to get in.

"Talk? About what?"

"Nothing. Books. Stories. People."

I would say anything to shut him up. I was exhausted and dying to get some sleep. His insistent whispering so close was worse than the heat, the flies, and the lack of a breeze.

"Do you kiss her?"

"No!" Disgusted. That ought to stop him.

"Did you ever kiss anyone? Not your mother or father or Grandpa either."

"Sure," I said, vaguely remembering a party some months before around the block from where we lived. Boys and girls had coupled off into a dark basement littered with large unused furniture. We had blankly and almost blindly kissed each other until we were breathless and panting.

"Who?" Chas asked. He was sitting on the edge of his bed now, his interest audibly intensified now instead of lessened.

"Some girl. No one important."

"Did you feel her teats?"

I tried to remember. "Yeah."

"What were they like?"

"I don't know. Small. Soft."

"Did she like it?"

"What? Kissing?"

"No! Touching her teats?"

"I guess."

"Did you let her touch you?"

"No."

"Why not?"

"I don't know. I just didn't."

I turned over and moved closer to the wall. The wrong move. Instead of Chas going back to sleep, he

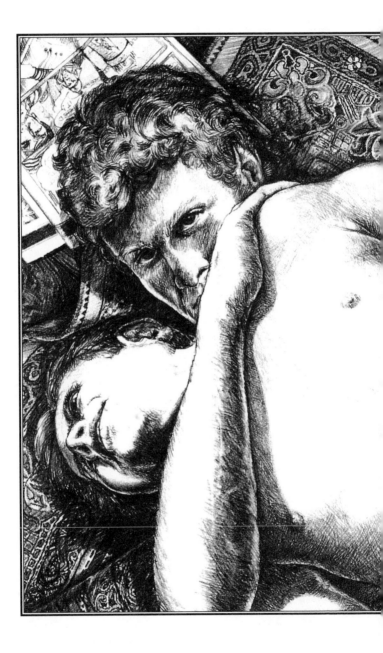

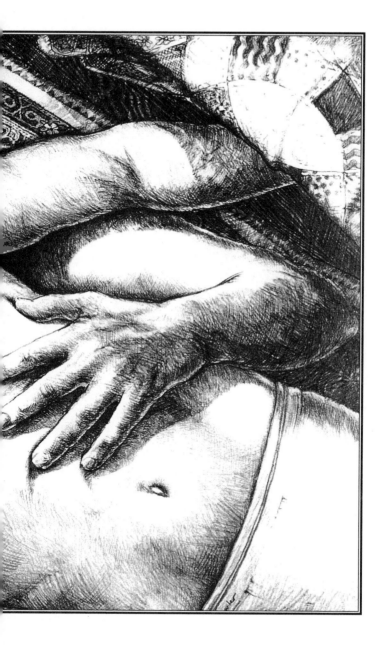

came into my bed. I could sense him almost touching my back. He whispered closer now, his breath steamy against the back of my neck.

"Did you touch her?"

"I said I did."

"No. Down there." To illustrate, he put his hands around me, across my thighs right under where my underpants stopped.

"No."

"I did," he said.

"Oh, yeah?" As bored as I could make it sound.

"Yeah! And more. I did more than just touch." He hadn't moved his hands and was now rubbing them gently back and forth. I felt more than heard him doing something behind me.

"How does this feel?" he asked. His voice sounded so grown-up that I half turned around to check that it was really only Chas there.

"Take this off. It's too hot," he said, doing it for me. "Only babies wear underwear. I don't. Feel."

I reached over, languidly brushing the hot skin of his stomach. He gripped my hand there.

"What are you doing?" I asked.

"It feels good, doesn't it?"

"It's OK."

"You ever do this before?"

"No."

"And you never had anyone do it to you?" His voice had risen again, almost to normal.

"No."

"That's what girls will do for you. I've had it done a lot. Now you do it to me too."

"I can't reach behind me," I said, and he rolled over me until we were now facing each other. He still held on to me, while he arranged my hand in a loose fist and pushed himself into it. His other arm circled my waist and moved up and down my back, arms, stomach and legs. I began feeling hot and light-headed, cramped yet not uncomfortable.

"How does *that* feel?" he asked again in a whisper even more hoarse than before. I wanted to tell him that I wasn't feeling right and that he ought to stop it. All that came out of me was a small sigh.

He nuzzled into my neck then. In a second he was trying to kiss me. I wanted to push him off me, but I was feeling so oddly languorous and hot, I couldn't bring myself to make him stop what he was doing.

"This is a French kiss," he whispered into my ear. This time he forced my mouth open and nearly pulled my breath out of me, pushing and rubbing faster and faster against me with his hands. "This is what you do with girls," he said, and he was moving at such a rate, I thought there was no stopping him.

I was getting dizzy. Where his hands were, I was beginning to sweat and to even feel sore, but he was as maniacally energetic as I wasn't, and I let him do what he was doing until I began feeling a new sensation, so much like burning needles all over my lower front that I began to gasp and found the energy to push him away for a second.

"Leave it!" he hissed.

"Stop. Let go!" I whispered back.

But he wouldn't. And now the burning got so bad I began to whimper.

"Don't. Stop."

"Leave it! I'll do it for you."

I tried twisting away from him, but he still held on to me. Like burning needles all up and down my front, getting hotter, seeming to move in patterns all across my stomach and legs. Until I felt I couldn't stand it anymore and whispered, "It hurts! It hurts!"

"Now!" he whispered angrily, pushing himself into my hand so hard, I had to hold the edge of the bed with the other hand to get some semblance of balance.

"Ah!" I began to cry as it welled up and out of me. "Chas! It hurts!"

I leaped off the bed, getting away from him by this surprise movement. It came welling up and over me again and again as I stood against the wall, feeling as if I were falling down a flight of stairs. "What did you do to me?"

But Chas lay back panting and writhing around on the bed, oblivious to me.

Finally it subsided, and I reached down and touched myself. Then I was really frightened. It was all wet.

"Blood," I said half aloud and ran out of the bedroom and into the bathroom.

Seconds later Chas was standing there beside me.

"Look" I said, feeling terrified. I'd never seen anything like it.

"What's wrong?" he said angrily.

"Look! You broke it or something. What's all this?"

"Hush up, stupid!" he said, then closed the bathroom door behind him. He looked down at me, laughing. "You mean to say that never happened to you before?"

"No. I told you to stop. Look what happened."

"Never?" he asked. "Never? Never?"

"What's wrong with it?"

"There's nothing wrong with it," he sneered, imitating me. "Come on. Let's go back to the bedroom before someone comes to see what's going on."

"No, don't," I said. He'd put his arm around me again.

"Why not?"

"I don't know. I'm afraid."

"Of what? It's supposed to do that, dummy. Come on back to bed. I'll show you."

"I don't want to."

"Don't be a baby. I won't touch you. I'll show you on

myself. You want to grow up sometime, don't you? You'll have to know about this, you know."

Patiently—because of my many hesitations—in that next hour or so, he showed me the entire repertoire of activities to be engaged in alone or with someone else. I saw the same thing happen to him that had happened to me, and so I wasn't terrified anymore. After a while I could even begin to feel the pleasure of his touch on my body again. Then he showed me how to do it to him. Watching his face and hearing his moans made me feel that I had some power over Chas for the first time since I'd met him, and so gave an added edge of pleasure to that which I couldn't really explain.

"You've still got a lot to learn," Chas said some time later, after turning over on his back to go to sleep in his own bed. "A real lot. And I'm going to show it to you."

I lay back too, unable to sleep, my mind a jumble of thoughts, my body feeling as though it belonged to someone else. My body felt so odd after so many different new sensations. I was in awe of it: its newly revealed areas of sensitivities, its completely unexpected capabilities. Even more awesome was the ease with which I had been able to produce similar previously unknown sensitivities in someone else's body.

It was as though the bedroom walls had fallen down on either side of me—I was so exposed. I turned to Chas to tell him all this. But he was already asleep, his light hair curling wildly over his face, his body stretched on its side so pale that it looked like a freshly killed game cat I'd once seen slung across the fender of a hunter's car.

I had to lean over him to make sure he was still alive. Then, when I was certain he was breathing, even lightly snoring, I got back into my own bed. Even with the terrific heat, I began to shiver so much that I had to pull on a blanket. I knew I would never be able to tell Chas what had happened to me, and that made me want to cry all the more: knowing I would never be able to express how my universe had changed.

5

I was finally able to get to sleep—having to be awakened for breakfast, instead of being up a half hour before, as usual. Bleary-eyed, I noticed that nothing else besides myself had changed in the world. Not even—most surprisingly—Chas. He didn't refer in any way to what had occurred between us and never gave me any real chance to talk about it, as he disappeared soon after breakfast and didn't return home until dinner was already on the table. Nor, later on, when we were both in bed, did he say a word about it. He merely made sure the door was closed, then came to my bed with as much heat and intensity as the night before, leaving me shaking and shivering once more, longing for sleep and comfort.

Thus began a curious life for me, split between the daytime—a world of beaches and hikes, ice creams, the library, and fishing with Grandpa—and the night, a

world of hot hands, sweating limbs, twisted sheets, des-
perate kisses and caresses, whispered obscenities, pre-
tended and even some real affections, passions, and
hurts. Only later on would I come to see this night
world as the tissue of involuntary degeneracy it actually was. For the moment I was so caught up in it by the
sudden release of unknown feelings within me, I could
think of nothing but of mine and Chas's pleasure, how
to accomplish it, and how often.

Chas's attitude toward our nights certainly determined how I took them: He was cautious, always closing the door to the hallway, always shushing me if he
thought we were making too much noise. But he never
hinted at the possibility (later, only later, how well understood!) that what we were doing was wrong. We
were merely doing what other boys our age did; something parents didn't know about, or if they did, didn't
want to know about from us. For all I knew then, it was
perfectly natural, even when most painful; innocent,
even when I was feeling most clearly disgraced. As a
topic, our nights were banned from daytime discus-
sions; and, as they only led to more of the same when
brought up at night, I had no point of reference, no
value system to set them in.

I knew from Chas that he and the Muller boys had
done the same. He even suggested that he and I go to
their place one day and he'd show me. But he never

did. As far as girls doing it also, which he strongly hinted at, it seemed at best unlikely to me, and given what
little I knew of their different anatomies, almost irrele-
vant. Certainly I couldn't see my sister or his or Eileen
(not to mention Mother or Aunt Linda) engaging in
any such activities. Eileen especially was so cool and
fresh and calm all the time, I believed she could never
become so sweaty and frenzied as we did nightly. No,
this was clearly out of her range. Whereas the older
women were so large, so ungainly, as to make most of
our more common methods of mutual gratification im-
possible to perform.

So there we were, Chas and I, in my new universe,
and I couldn't help but feel he was only partly there.
Certainly at night he was—alternately aggressive and
tender, bursting with ideas and methods of drawing
out or raising up our levels of pleasure to unthought of,
unprepared for, all-encompassing tension and release.

In the daytime he was merely Chas, my cousin, with
his previous abilities and still unexplained mysteries,
with his casualness and taste for mischief that remained
unchanged. He was only a boy, a year or two older than
me, and in many ways more ignorant than me, despite
his continued scorn and impatience for what he saw as
my inferior abilities.

After these nights together had begun, Chas and I
were together more during the day, even though this

togetherness had little of the depth of connection we made at night. We would be wrestling on the lawn or engaged in acrobatics in the surf. But our physical contact in these daytime activities was merely that: contact, with none of the incredible power that hours later a single fingertip drawn across a sternum or rib cage would produce.

Nevertheless, we were seen as a pair, and this affected those around us. Mother—who'd paid very little attention to me so far this summer (luckily!)—now began criticizing my being away from the house so much and finding all sorts of chores for me to do to stay closer. Janet and Cathy no longer asked me to walk them to the stores on Twill Road after dinner, afraid, I suppose, that I would begin bullying them. Grandpa—who never seemed too much to care for Chas before—now made certain to ask him along on the few expeditions we took in the area. I even had the strange experience of a housemaid, five doors away from ours, rushing out at me into the middle of the street, trying to swat at me with her broom and loudly accusing me of tying her cat to a picket fence.

Most of all, Eileen changed. I began seeing less and less of her because I was seeing more of Chas, but she and I still managed a few hours two or three days a week for an ice cream, a walk to the library, and a talk. Occasions that became almost formal for me, as she grew more distant from me—except for one outburst on her part, when she declared Chas "a bad influence on me," a phrase I was certain she had picked up from some grown-up and which led me to defend him at great length.

What made it worse was that I knew he wasn't helping me. I allowed myself to go along with Chas in several dubious adventures. We had a rock fight with some boys our age on a farm adjoining the town and didn't leave until one of the boys had been hit in the head and was bleeding. We'd gone up to the Indian's treaty rock and smoked cigarettes Chas had bought in town until we were both dizzy. We took an unannounced and later punished hitchhike ride to Scituate, where we spent all day hanging around trying to make trouble with the local kids, until we'd spotted a Flash Gordon serial at the movies and snuck in, getting home late.

Even if I didn't enjoy these forays into wild boyhood very much, I still would have given up Eileen, Grandpa, the library, ice cream, my entire family for Chas—Chas at night, that is.

And if I ever felt doubts, he made sure of my continued loyalty by his infrequently but precisely timed gestures. If before I used to be made uncomfortable whenever I would catch Chas staring idly at me, now I knew that what he was doing was not idle; he was seeing in his mind what I had done with him only hours before or planning for that night. He would laugh his grown-up chuckle, then roll over on his back, scratching on the grass like a dog in the sand. Or while we were walking somewhere, he would put his hand on the back of my neck, a finger and thumb slightly pressing on either side, as if to show me how completely in possession of me he was.

He did that one Sunday afternoon, all the way back to Grandpa Lynch's house from a boring, childish birthday party we'd been invited to and left early. Finding no one at home yet—they'd gone for a drive to Groton and the Coast Guard station—Chas and I had gone into the refrigerator for sandwich makings, then he'd gotten that look of intensity on his face and suggested, persuaded, and finally insisted we go up to our bedroom to do with the blinds closed and the gray afternoon shut out what we'd so often done only during the night.

That was the afternoon I realized that I could not deny Chas anything he wanted from me, the day I realized he had made a slave of me, just as he said he would during that first meeting, when he sucked the blood from my hand.

This came over me only after he had left the shuttered bedroom to wander off. The others had returned, and I went to sit out on the shore-side deck of the veranda, trying to read, failing, and pretending I wasn't as terrified as I felt I really was of Chas's hold over me.

Only Grandpa Lynch seemed to notice something was wrong with me that evening. While he was always too tactful to ask what bothered me, he stayed close to me the rest of the day so that I could at least feel the safety and comfort of his presence.

It helped, and I so much wanted it to continue that after our large Sunday dinner, as we sat back out on the veranda watching the sun begin to drop its orange ball from a blue clear sky into an equally blue ocean, I asked Grandpa Lynch to tell me a story, a true story about real people.

Grandpa looked at me and said he knew a true story, but that it was a long and involved story, did I think I was grown up enough to want to sit through it and try to understand it? It concerned Amity Pritchard and the Pritchard place.

Chas was leaning against the wall of the house, playing solitaire with the cards laid out on the planking in front of him. He said he was ready to hear it. So, I too begged Grandpa to tell me everything he knew about Amity Pritchard, everything, because I'd rather hear the truth—even if I didn't understand all of it—than a story only told for children that hid the truth.

Grandpa must have understood my troubled mind then, because he filled up the pipe he always carried in the upper left-hand pocket of his shiny-with-age gray vest, lit it, and, puffing on it, slowly looked at me. He saw my pain and fear and uncertainty, and he began to speak.

6

I met Amity Pritchard only one time in my life, he said, when I was about eight years old; so don't expect me to tell you about her character or anything like that. I got impressions of her. I won't say that I didn't. But I can't say how much they were colored by what I already knew of her from hearing others talk. Because even then there was plenty of talk about Amity Pritchard, although their property wasn't all deserted and gone to ruin like it is now. Still, I did meet the woman—the lady, I should say, because she was a lady, the finest and of the first family in the entire county, even though she had been brought low by her particular destiny. But there she was, just as close as you are to me, and that's a whole lot closer than many of those who talked about her could say, who never even laid eyes on her, or on the property, except from Atwood Avenue, much as they liked to shoot off their mouths about it.

Amity was wearing all black, I recall. A big black hat of the kind I believe women then called schooners, on account of they were so long and tall they took the wind like a set of sails at sea. Veils all over that hat; pointed veils like you don't see anymore. And black clothing too. A short, jacket-like top coming down to her hips over a long black skirt right down to her feet, and a silk frilled front filling out the jacket at her throat and cuffs.

It was all that black that made me notice her. It was not a funeral we were attending but a christening, and black is out of character at a christening—except for the preacher who does the baptizing. But Amity was always in black—at least that's what I heard people saying.

The child being christened that morning was a cousin's son, which was why Amity was there. I recall everyone was sort of surprised to see her, even though it was her cousin's first child at the font. They were Todds—on her mother's side, the same people who now own the Pritchard place, although none of them ever lived there—but in Arizona, or California, or somewhere out West for the past thirty years.

As it was the first time anyone in town had seen Amity for five years, the first time since her misfortune, all the women were somewhat amazed that she came. It turned out to be the last time she ever left the Pritchard place too. A year later, she passed on in a

most violent manner, as you can discover yourself just
by reading the inscription on her stone in the Nansquett graveyard.

There were still one or two servants at her house
then; a grizzled old Nigrah, older than I am now, which
is considerably old, was driving the carriage that Amity
came to the chapel in. There were no cars then. That
was long before automobiles. All the servants were for-
mer slaves from the Southern states who'd run away
before the Confederate War, as Amity's father, the Reverend Pritchard, had been an abolitionist. Nobody ever
knew how many of them were still on the place when
Amity died. Some people said ten, and some a hundred. No one ever went near there after '68, even
though Amity was still alive and it didn't have the reputation it's gotten attached to it since. I believe there
was only one Nigrah, the older driver named Saturn,
who was deaf and ready to die and didn't mind staying
around, even though Amity was known to be crazy and
wild and melancholic since the misfortune with her sister and that Union captain, Eugene V. Calder.

She stood right by me, three rows back from the
christening font, not at front with the rest of the Todd
family, so I got a good enough view of her, even with
her veils. What I saw made me suspect people didn't
know what they were talking about. Amity didn't look
at all wild; not crazy at all; not even sad. She was still

a youngish woman then—in her prime, and with an almost porcelain-white complexion, lips and cheeks and temples as white as anything I'd ever seen. Ladies did not go out in the sun in those days, except with a parasol. The only other remarkable thing about her were her eyes—blue eyes, so pale and blue they might have been like the sky on a sunny day. A pale blue, but strong too, and surrounded by tiny yellow lashes that made them stand out even more. Quiet eyes. Quiet and calm. I know they calmed me, when she looked at me, and then put one of her hands—gloved in black lace like her veils—on my shoulder, as though to steady herself standing there, during the ceremony. I kept looking up at her—amazed myself that this supposedly wild woman had such a young clear face and such quiet eyes.

Amity didn't stay long at the christening, not as long as for the dinner afterward. Instead, as soon as everyone gathered around the Todds to congratulate them, she leaned over me, took a small package out of a lacy black reticule hanging off one of her wrists, and pressed it into my hand, whispering to ask me to lay the tiny damask gift alongside the other gifts for the baby. When I had and had come back to the pew, she was gone from the vestry.

I went to the door then and just caught sight of her getting into the big carriage. Once settled in her seat,

she seemed to notice me on the church steps and motioned me over. "Did you lay down the gift?" she asked
me in a voice as deep and calm as any I'd heard from
the preacher himself. "Yes, ma'am," I answered her.
"Here then," she said, "this is for being so good," and
she reached into that reticule and pulled out an Eagle
and put it into my hand. That's a five-dollar gold piece.

It glittered so in the afternoon sun. I was surprised
to see more money than I'd ever seen in my life, and I
guess my mouth must have fallen open. "Don't tell anyone I gave it to you," she said then. "Don't tell anyone
until you're a grown man. Then go and spend it on
something foolish—on a woman is best. Some foolish
trinket for a woman. Do you understand me?" Without
waiting for an answer, she tapped on the side of the
carriage, and Saturn drove her away. That was the last
I saw of her.

I never did tell anyone about the Eagle she gave me.
I hid it in the Bible I'd been given, the same Bible I
have upstairs. Ten years later, when I was on my own in
Boston, I spent the money just as Amity told me to, to
take a woman to dinner and a concert of the Sympho-
ny Orchestra.

Several times after that I went near the road to her
house, off Atwood Avenue, but I never did go all the
way up to her house. And a year later, she was dead.

It was only at her funeral that I found out more

about her; and only some twenty years after that, when I was studying to be an attorney at law, and was conversing with retired Judge Wilcomb, that I heard how it was that such a beautiful woman, so well-bred and well-off, came to be living alone years on end with nothing but one old Nigrah servant to tend her, and came to be feared and shunned and ostracized by the entire county.

It hadn't always been so—and I guess that was all the more of a surprise to people. As I said, Amity came from the finest, the most prosperous of families. The Pritchards had been merchant seamen for several generations, living and operating out of Salem and later Providence and Bristol. But Amity's father had been the second son of the family, an ordained minister of God, and he had come here to Nansquett about the year 1830, like many other Providence folk who'd visited here in the summertime, and had come to enjoy the area. Reverend Pritchard bought a large parcel of land along Twill Road, from where the highway entrance is now down to the river, where the big mill was put up. That was north of Nansquett and south of Scituate—just right for his large parish. For he was a fine preacher, upstanding and fair for all of his youth when he came here, social and educated and more elegant than any preacher that had been encountered in the county. He married a Nansquett girl, Martha Todd, and when his first child, a boy, was born, he began to build the big house that is in dilapidation today.

That's where Amity was born in 1842, as her tombstone says; and three years later, her sister, Constance. Amity had an ordinary enough childhood, except that when she was just becoming a young woman, her brother—several years younger than Amity—caught scarlet fever and died. That upset old Calvin Pritchard more than it ought to have—children died of scarlet fever by the dozens every year. But he doted so much on his son and must have taken it as a judgment on himself from God, because of his pride. He was a religious man—as the girls' names attest—and now he became almost obsessively religious, leaving more and more of his pastoral duties to his assistant minister and staying locked up in the big library at the top of the Pritchard house, poring over the testaments and the Apocrypha, trying to glean reasons for his afflictions.

The girls' lives didn't change very much. Their mother still considered herself the county's social dictator, and they were better educated than was usual in those days, learning French and German, studying poetry and philosophy even, considered heavy going even for young men. Constance didn't take much to this studying, but Amity did. She had a distinctly intellectual bent, and would amaze her young men callers with her facts and ideas and questions.

Both girls did begin to have callers in profusion, especially Amity, who was the elder and the more eligible. For besides being so learned, she had all of the more social graces—knowing how to play the piano and how to sing Mendelssohn and Meyerbeer songs with the best of the big-city women. She was always the first to suggest and invent entertainments, always the first to lead a waltz at the infrequent balls that were given in the area. Many young men confessed themselves struck to adoration by Amity. Including both of my own uncles. It was no surprise therefore when her engagement to Alfred Wilcomb was announced.

For all of her popularity, however, people were quick to notice that as far as her sister was concerned, Amity was devoted almost to the point of blindness. Although Constance was as pretty as Amity, she was far less liked and considered scheming and vixenish. She seemed to enjoy irritating, deceiving, frustrating, and humiliating her own smitten suitors. And her criticism of her rivals—including Amity—was both painful and accurate. Amity seemed not to mind a bit. She wouldn't brook an unkind word against her sister and defended her staunchly. She sacrificed social affairs and friends alike to her sister, and instead of going out, spent as much time as possible with her. Constance was temperamental, flighty, and capricious. And Amity adored the ground she trod on. Folks just shook their heads and said no good would come of it, that Amity had best marry Wilcomb and get away from her family as soon as possible.

This proved difficult, for no sooner were the guns at Fort Sumter sounded than Amity's fiancé volunteered for the Union Army. Many other young men joined up too, for war was glorious at that time, and the tradition against slavery was especially strong in this county, among Reverend Pritchard's parishioners. Amity was as supportive of his decision as anyone else, believing that the war would be over in a few months at most and then she and Alfred could marry.

It wasn't to be. Alfred was killed by a common shot at Manassas two years later; and Amity began to wear black for the first time. She was almost never to be able to remove it again, for scarcely was her mourning for Wilcomb over when her mother passed on. Then the Reverend died, and later on the others followed him to the grave.

No one seems to know when Captain Eugene V. Calder first met Amity. Telling me later on, Judge Wilcomb said that Calder had been instructed by Alfred to deliver a final letter to his fiancée. It wasn't until after General Lee had surrendered at Appomattox in 1865 that Calder arrived in Nansquett with this letter. He stayed with his friend's family. The judge, a boy of eighteen, remembered Calder as decorated, dashing, eloquent, and gentlemanly beyond reproach.

Evidently Amity thought so too, for she soon allowed him to visit her—ostensibly to talk about and to commiserate on the loss of her fiancé and his friend. When it was suggested to Calder that his stay in Nansquett seemed prolonged to the point of seeming to be a courtship, he denied it. A proud man, he went his own way in all he did: typical, people here said, of a Vermonter, for he was a White Mountain–bred man, and they are known to be an ornery, independent lot.

However much Calder denied his wooing, those who visited with Amity knew otherwise. She had bloomed as never before since Eugene Calder had come to Nansquett. The three terrible years of death and loss had passed, leaving in their wake a sense that all was for the best. If she had lost one good man, she had found a better one. She intimated to friends that as soon as her mourning period for her father was over, she would be dressed in the whitest of white. Calder needn't buy land or look for an occupation. With the Reverend gone, it was all Amity and her steward could do to keep managing their farm and house. That she and Calder would be wed was soon accepted by everyone in the county, and no one was anything but pleased by it, for Amity was loved and respected by just about all then, and her own indisputable sorrows in a time of sorrow were much deplored.

I guess it's wrong to say everyone was pleased with the courtship. Constance wasn't, although we weren't to find that out until after Calder had gone up to Vermont and returned again to Nansquett.

He was gone about eight months, which in those days of slow travel and communications was unsurprising, especially as all assumed he was closing his own affairs and readying himself for his new life. But the time of waiting began to tell on Amity. She ceased visiting as much as she had; almost, people thought, as though to avoid naturally curious questioning about her wedding plans. Nothing was settled. She would wait until Calder returned to announce their marriage, she said. When pressed on it, she would start acting strange, make jokes, become irritable—something no one had ever noticed in her before. It was about then that the postmaster let it out that Amity had received only two letters from Vermont and that her sister, Constance, had gotten more than a dozen.

When Captain Calder returned to Nansquett, it was much later than anyone had thought—summer instead of winter. He didn't stay at the Scituate hotel or at the Wilcombs' house as before but went right up to the Pritchard house—which astonished and scandalized a great many people. But it also made them certain the marriage would come off as expected. Or would it?

For suddenly it was no longer Amity riding alongside

Captain Calder in the open carriage but Constance. As
Amity was not going out calling anymore, a few of her
family's closer friends went to see her. At first they did
see her—but she wouldn't satisfy them about the curious turn of Calder's affections. Whenever anyone became too insistent with her, Amity—always a lady—
would excuse herself from the best parlor, saying she
felt faint or was coming down with a migraine
headache. This might have been accepted as mere ec-
centricity, but more than one such rebuffed visitor
passed out of the hallway onto the big front porch,
where Captain Calder might be seen reading to Constance aloud, or their singing and laughter would trickle out of the music room into the foyer. Soon Amity
wasn't receiving any visitors at all.

Then the banns were called, and half the congrega-
tion of Reverend Pritchard's church were stunned to
hear that it was the younger sister the Captain was
going to marry that June. The other half—more in the
know, although just as scandalized—merely turned to
each other with looks that said "I told you so."

May came and went, and no one saw or heard anything of Calder or the Pritchard girls. Then it was settled once and for all: Constance and the Captain fore-
seeing the unavoidable scandal of a large, public
wedding, went for a week to visit her aunt and uncle in
Bristol, and got married there. The way in which this

was revealed was simple enough—a copy of their wedding registration was delivered to the Nansquett Justice of the Peace, who did just as he was supposed to do in such matters and posted it on the office board and then had it published in the county weekly newspaper.

There was a great deal of talk for some months, then everyone seemed to accept the fact. Not that the Captain and Constance received much company from town. They didn't. Nor did they begin calling on folks either. Strangest of all, Amity hadn't been seen in months—she'd taken ill, some of the servants answered when closely questioned by relations, and had remained ill.

This was in 1867. Their situation remained about the same for over a year. Then it came to an unexpected and climactic explosion.

It was the Negro servant Saturn who told everything to the Wilcombs. Captain and Mrs. Calder had been killed when their carriage had overturned and crashed into a ditch at the turning to the Boston Post Road, on their way to Scituate. Amity had been told of their deaths, but hadn't reacted at all. Someone had to come claim the bodies.

Naturally, everyone in town was shocked. The Post Road was a safe and level enough stretch, even in bad weather. Calder wasn't known as a reckless driver. The horses pulling the carriage were old and tame, not quick to shy at trouble; they hadn't been hurt in the accident. When Wilcomb and his father reached the scene of the deaths, just off the highway exit now from Nansquett, they saw what had happened—two wheels of the carriage on the right side had snapped off. Evidently suddenly, and at the same time. Unable to deal with this in the moonlit night, the Captain had probably reined in too tight, and everything had gone over. He was still alive, his skull fractured by the sideboard, blood gushing out of it onto the grass, when they were found next morning. He died as the sun rose, his final words incomprehensible. Constance, it appeared, had died instantly.

Now Amity came out of her seclusion. If the town hadn't the splendid wedding it felt it had deserved from her, it got the largest and most magnificent double funeral it had ever expected to see. Husband and wife were interred together in the Pritchard family plot, and Amity was cordial and magnificently genteel in her sorrow. People talked, but people always talk when the unexpected occurs. Ready as folks were to commiserate with her, others also had a malicious delight in the double death, as though that was the only thing to be expected for the obviously errant couple.

Slowly, months later, gradually, almost quietly, like water seeping out of a deteriorating dike, the word began to be nosed around the county that the deaths might not have been completely accidental. The Pritchard's livery servant, who'd been since dismissed from his job and taken to lurking about Scituate, claimed foul play. He'd cared for the carriage, he said, and there had been nothing wrong with it, and if there had been, it was someone else's doing. Lord knew, he said, there were some people who'd been oppressed long enough to want to get revenge, and he didn't mean black folk either.

Rumors soon began to run so fast that an investigation was finally made into the matter. The carriage was inspected, but as it had been repaired months before, that did no good or harm. It was clear to all the women in town that if the accident had been intentional only one person held a motive for it—Amity. But whether she—or any woman—knew enough about such mechanical devices, no one could declare with certainty.

Nothing ever came of the investigation, but Amity was tried, defended, and convicted in public opinion. She knew it. While after the funeral she had begun tentatively to socialize again with her closest old acquaintances, she now became completely reclusive, never coming into town, sending her Negro Saturn for needed provisions. The few white servants still remaining were dismissed, and soon the Pritchard house became as though a blight had struck it.

People still talked about her, of course; some claimed

to have seen Amity wandering disheveled through the woods adjoining the house, shrieking and tearing her hair out of her head in great clumps from guilt and remorse. Others claimed that she and her remaining servants held all sorts of secret rites and orgies at the house on nights of a full moon. No one knew anything for certain; all was speculation and fancy. And soon, no one really cared. Amity had become a total recluse, whatever her reasons for doing so and however she actually passed her time. As a recluse she was easily categorized and so accepted in the town's limited view of the world.

Naturally, mothers threatened naughty children with her, as though she were a witch or a bogey. So we all grew up knowing her name and knowing there was something terrible about her. God knows, at worst, she was a tormented murderess, though more than likely she was nothing more than a woman battered time and again by a hostile fate. But who knew for certain? Even I—who'd been so taken with her at the christening—couldn't say for certain if Amity hadn't loosened the bolts on those carriage wheels the night Constance and Captain Calder died.

Nor did I ever have the chance to find out. As I said, a year or so after our meeting, her servant Saturn came and knocked on the Justice of the Peace's door and led a half-dozen men up to the Pritchard place. That morning he'd missed his mistress, searched the house and grounds for her, and not found her. Spooked by this, he'd finally, slowly begun his daily chores, one of which was to draw up enough water from the well for the cooking and laundering.

Floating face up in the well was Amity. No one had to explain her reasons or the probable course of events. She'd merely followed her evil destiny to its final re-morse-driven end. Naturally, with a life like hers—with a death like hers—people began to think the Pritchard property was haunted. All I know is that the house was closed up then, and no one has lived in it ever since then. The Todds inherited it all and sold off some of the land closest to Scituate, but none of them ever lived in the house or made any move to change or restore it. They still own it, I'm told, but it does them little good now, as the older Todds are all dead and the younger ones live half a continent away.

Still, tales about Amity are told to this day. Some claim to see strange greenish lights in the house at night, although how they ever got close enough to see is beyond me, since it's a good 300 yards in off Atwood Avenue and so overgrown, most folks would be fool-hardy to walk there at night. But such tales will persist, especially when there is nothing to stop them.

That, to my knowledge, is Amity's story, boy. You asked, and I told you, omitting nothing I heard.

7

"You mean, there's no ghost there?" I had to ask.

"None that I know of," Grandpa said.

I turned to look at Chas, to see how he was taking this contradiction. But it was already so dark, I couldn't see his face.

"Chas saw a ghost there," I said.

Grandpa didn't say anything.

"At least, that's what Chas told me."

I heard Chas get up and open the screen door to the house.

"There is one," he said, whispering it. "There is!" Then he went in.

Grandpa Lynch and I sat silent out on the shore-side deck for a long time until the low-lying clouds that had remained pink long after the sun had set were swallowed up into the general deep blue of the night sky.

Then Mother came to call me in to bed.

I kissed Grandpa good night right there and thanked him for telling the story. I wasn't sure how much of it I understood: passions of the intensity he had told were so new to me, I wasn't sure they could be powerful enough to change people's lives as they had apparently changed Amity's and her sister's.

"You liked Amity, didn't you?" I asked Grandpa.

"I liked her well enough. But what can a boy know. I can't say that I would have liked her if I were older when I met her."

As I didn't know what he meant by that, I let it ride and went up to my bedroom. Chas was undressed, sitting in his bed with the little light on, reading a Batman comic. He didn't look up when I came in and got ready for sleep. I lay down and thought about Amity and how sad her life had been. I wondered if my own life would ever become remarkable enough for people to talk about it almost a hundred years after. Maybe. Maybe if I did something great, like being the first man on Mars or inventing a medicine to keep people from dying.

While I was thinking, Chas finished with his comic book and shut off his light. I suddenly felt that I didn't want him to come to my bed that night. I wanted to be alone with my thoughts of Amity and of the future, possible me.

"Chas?" I asked tentatively, intending to ask him if he would mind putting off what we did at night.

"I'm tired," he said, his voice muffled in the pillow. "Go to sleep."

That was a relief. "Are you sore?"

"There is too a ghost," he said. "I'll show you."

"But Grandpa said—"

"What does he know? He's never been there. He's too yellow to go. For all his talk."

That irritated me. "Well, I'm not yellow," I said. "Show me. Show me tomorrow."

"I will. But it's got to be at night. She won't be there until it gets dark. So that's when we have to go."

"How?"

"I don't know. We'll make up some excuse. We'll say we're going to get an ice cream and see your girlfriend."

"Well, whatever she is."

"We'll go there after dinner. We have to pass the Pritchard place anyway, don't we?"

"I guess."

"Are you backing out already?"

"I'll go. I just don't like lying," I said. Or dragging Eileen's name into lying either, I wanted to say.

"We won't be lying, if we go to see her," Chas said. "Just not telling everything. We don't tell everything we do together anyway. Do we?"

"I guess not."

Chas laughed. "You *bet* we don't." He leaned over onto my bed.

"I thought you wanted to go to sleep," I said.

"*You* don't. Look at *that*," he said, touching me.

So we got into it anyway—hollow as it felt to me that night, with my thoughts everywhere else but on what we were doing.

When we were done and Chas had gone back to his own bed, I said, "Chas? Do you think that Amity Pritchard really did turn the bolts on that carriage?"

"She went and threw herself into that well, didn't she?" he said.

"She might have fallen in."

"In broad daylight?"

"Well, maybe. Maybe it wasn't in daylight. Maybe she was walking around at night and fell in."

"And maybe elephants have wings," he said. "She didn't fall in—and she did loosen those wheel bolts. That's why she's a ghost. She can't settle down like other dead people, because she feels bad about what she did."

"Would you ever do something like that, because you loved someone so hard?" I asked.

He sat up in his bed, and I could see his figure turned to me.

"Would you?" he asked.

"I don't think so. I don't think I could ever love anyone that hard," I finally said.

"Well, I'm not so sure of that. Now, good night."

I pondered a while on what he meant by that, but failing to find any satisfactory answer, I had to content myself with thinking again about being the first man on Mars.

Around dawn I woke up and looked around for the noise that had just awakened me. Chas was sitting up in bed.

"What's wrong, Chas?" I asked.

"Nothing. Go to sleep."

"Why aren't you asleep?"

"I had to go to the bathroom. Go to sleep."

"What's that in your hand?" I thought I'd seen something.

"A comic book. I'm reading it to tire out my eyes. Go to sleep." He turned around in bed, away from me.

I was to recall that sleepless night of his years later.

8

We didn't go to the Pritchard place the following night as we had planned.

My father came up to Nansquett to take his own vacation that day, and for the next two weeks he and I spent a great deal of time together. We went to drive-in movies, we took a ferry across the Providence River, which was as wide as a bay and went to Newport and even into Massachusetts, up to Salem. He drove us up to the amusement park at Scarborough Beach. We even went out to Block Island, sleeping over. It was fun for me, not only because I hadn't seen father in months and had missed him, but because he was unspoiled by all the weeks of familiarity I had with Nansquett and its environs. So, I was able to take him around, as Grandpa had taken me around earlier. I showed him the best fishing spots. I told him the best times to go clamming and crabbing, just before the tide came in again, when the beach was filled with tide pools teeming with oceanic life. I showed him how I'd learned to swim, and we raced across the river and back.

So it was almost September, almost time for all of us to leave Nansquett and for me to return to school, when Chas and I did finally make any definite plan to go to see Amity's ghost.

This turned out easier to carry off than it would have been earlier. First, it was suddenly getting darker much earlier every night than at the height of the summer. Where before we would sometimes go to sleep at night with some daylight still slipping under the venetian blinds of our room, these nights it was dark by eight o'clock—right after dinner—and we didn't have to go to bed until ten.

Easier still, because we had already begun going over to Eileen's store for that last ice cream of the day while Father was still in Nansquett. Partly this was because Chas realized that if he were going to live in Nansquett all year 'round beginning in September, when Aunt Linda and Uncle Al's house would be ready to be moved into, that he'd better start knowing a few more folks in town, especially a few more children he'd be going to school with and playing with during the fall and winter.

Eileen knew them all. And they all seemed to congregate around the ice-cream store in the hours between seven and nine at night, when the store closed.

I got to see another side of Chas in those few weeks as he set out to meet these children. Where I had always known him to be abrupt, opinionated, superior to and irritated by anyone else his age, they got to meet him as quiet, polite, smart, and very considerate.

Eileen told me she was surprised. She had misjudged Chas, she said, and was glad that I had defended him. I believed that Chas was acting this way just until he had them all in the palm of his hand, as I'd seen him do with other people, then he'd go back to being as he really was. Still, I couldn't be sure of that— couldn't be sure of anything concerning Chas, who remained as mysterious to me as Amity Pritchard was. So I kept my mouth shut. Eileen was intelligent enough to figure out what he was really like, I said to myself; why make trouble?

Our ghost hunt was planned for a Saturday night. We told our parents that we were going to help Eileen close her shop for the night, and help her move some large barrels her mother wanted put in the big outdoors refrigerator they shared with Millicent's grocery store. We said we'd probably be home later than usual, and no questions were asked. It was the last weekend of my stay in Nansquett, August 26, I recall, that Chas took me onto the Pritchard property to see Amity and my future.

Of course I didn't know that at the time. I thought
we were going to see a ghost, if Chas were telling the
truth—which I half doubted; hadn't Grandpa Lynch
said there was no ghost?

All afternoon and even during dinner, Chas kept
talking about how desolate the property was, and how
the house was set so far in from the road that if something terrible happened to us there, no one could ever
hear us screaming for help. We'd have to watch our
steps too, he said, as there was no light anywhere to
guide us. I suggested bringing a flashlight. But Chas
said no, we'd never see any ghost that way; it had to be
naturally dark.

By the time we'd turned off Atwood Avenue beyond
the bridge, all my doubts were subsiding into a wash
of anticipation. Chas kept talking about how we were
now on the road that edged one side of the Pritchard
property, and were probably already being watched by
the ghost. I was feeling sort of skittery.

Chas pointed out how dark it was. The almanac
Grandpa kept in the kitchen said the moon wouldn't
rise until after midnight. A few steps more, and I
knew we were at the entrance to the place. Not that
you could tell, really; it was as overgrown with bushes and brambles as any other part facing the avenue.
But I'd been on that spot many times before. There
was a telephone pole I had often marked as a land-

mark whenever I'd stopped to take a few steps in.

"Ready?" Chas asked.

I looked down Atwood Avenue to where the little bridge arched over the river and across to where the ice-cream store lights could be dimly seen. The asphalt on that part of the road gleamed in the streetlights' glare, making it look enormously far away. I felt myself looking there as though for a last-minute reprieve. All doubts about seeing the ghost had left me: I knew I was going to see something horrible, and I didn't want to.

"Well? Are you ready?" Chas asked again.

Before he could ask again, I stepped over the low bushes edging the road and onto the property. Chas joined me, and we began walking.

Even with the quickly fading light around us, we could make out that this had once been the driveway up to the house. Having seen it by daylight helped—I was familiar with it, at least for a hundred yards or so, before it turned sharply right to go uphill slightly, to the house. Tall trees lined the road, set closely together, as though purposely planted to afford shade, but nothing seemed to be growing on the dirt road in front of us. I could see two sets of deep ruts in the dirt, made by a wagon decades ago.

We walked on without speaking for a long time, until it seemed that the road came to an end; that was where it veered off, I suppose, to run a service road around the back of the house. I could hear Chas's shortened breathing a foot or so to my left. Without saying anything, I turned right with the dirt road and tried to make out the alleyway of trees. My eyes had adjusted to the darkness, but it seemed to be pitch black only a few yards ahead.

It was then that I heard an eerie whoosh on either side of me. Chas heard it too; he whispered, "The wind." That was followed by a sharp, mechanical-sounding cry and a rushing of wings just over our head. "Just a stupid bird," Chas said in that same hoarse whisper. "Let's go."

We continued on. It was dark but not dark enough to hide something darker still in the middle of the road. We stopped at the same time, then I walked up to it, staying off to one side and ready to dash off. It was the carcass of a dead animal—from the gleaming stripe down one side, a skunk. It smelled like month-old garbage. "Just an old skunk," Chas said and poked it with a stick.

We'd been walking so long I didn't know how far we had to go, when I began to hear the falling water. It sounded as though it was trickling down rocks. From what both Grandpa and Chas had said, I knew the Pritchard house was set up off the ground, approached by two sets of stone steps placed in a fieldstone retaining wall about eight feet high. The water must be coming from there, I thought. But it sounded all around me, not only from one direction—first to my right, then to my left, then straight ahead.

Chas must have heard the water too, even though he didn't say anything. It was such a clear trickling, the only distinct sound among the engulfing whoosh of the wind all about us—so clear a sound, it might have been inches away from me instead of yards off.

It was then that I sensed it was becoming less dark. Not that I could make out any real light. The foliage around us was still so thick above our heads, we couldn't make out a patch of starred night sky. But it was lighter—light enough to see the leaves of the trees, the dappled bark of their trunks, more ruts crossing and crisscrossing the dirt road: a sort of seeping light, as when daylight is an hour off but you still can see that it's coming.

With my sudden ability to see things because of the light, I felt better somehow. Curious too about where the light came from. Could someone be up at the house? Living there? Some vagabonds? That would be terrific. I walked on, it getting brighter, until the leaves of the trees suddenly gave way on either side and we were in a clearing covered with dirt road.

It was a large space, filled with that same strange light, which was oddly brighter in the center than on the sides. To my right I made out what seemed to be the doors of a barn or stable, where all of the ruts in the dirt yard crossed each other the most. This must have been where the carriages and wagons were kept, I thought. Across the yard from it were just more trees. But in between was a wall, and, feeling it gingerly, I made out huge chunks of rock set in mortar. The trickling water was clearest here, though no louder than before, and it had suddenly become windlessly quiet but for the trickling. I ran my hand over the rock wall until I reached some that were glossily wet. Then I moved along the wall until it gave way and I found one of the stairways up.

I was so entranced with my little discoveries that I was halfway up the steps when I remembered Chas. I turned around to find him.

"Chas!" I whispered.

Silence, then I heard, "Where are you?"

I followed the sound of his voice until I made out his figure, far away, standing with his stick held out in front of him, at the edge of the yard. His head turned from side to side, as though searching.

"I'm here!" I whispered loudly. "On the stairway. Come on."

"What are you doing?"

"I'm going up the stairs."

"What's that sound?"

"It's water. It's coming down the side of the wall."

"From the well?'"

"I don't know. Is the well up here?'"

"I think so."

"Don't you know?" I asked. "I thought you've been up here before."

Silence from him. Then, "Come on down."

"What for? We're this far. We might as well go right up and into the house." As Chas didn't answer, I urged him on. "Why are you waiting way over there?'"

"What's that light?" he asked me.

"I don't know. Aren't you coming?'"

"I don't like it," he said, and, distinct as his words were, his voice had a tremor in it. "It's not natural. I don't like it at all."

I felt sure he was still trying to scare me, so I said, "I'm going up the stairs and into the house." I wasn't afraid. Nor did I think Chas was afraid. He was just being silly. I had reached the top of the stairway and turned to face the dark mass of the big house some fifty feet in front of me. There seemed to be as much light up here as on the ground, although it didn't seem to come from anywhere in particular, certainly not from any windows in the house. The light seemed to hug the ground. With its aid I could see the front of the Pritchard house fairly well: the tall four-story turret and the big, flat three-story facade with its large entry and high dark windows. I could even make out smaller structures behind it, and the tottering bulk of rocks and wood off to one side, which must have been the well.

"Chas!" I whispered, "Chas! The well *is* up here. Come look."

Chas was standing exactly where I'd left him, still holding the stick, still looking around. I heard him say in what seemed to be a tiny voice, "I don't like it here. I don't!" He threw down the stick, spun around, and began running faster than I'd ever seen anyone run before.

"Chas!" I called after him, the first time I'd dared to raise my voice above a whisper. But he never looked back. He just ran until I couldn't see him anymore.

It was then that I had a moment of the sheerest terror of my life. What hadn't he liked? What had he seen or felt or heard that had made him refuse to come across the yard, that had made him run off? Terrified, I looked all around me, at the dark mass of the house looming, and I wondered, *What if he saw Amity's ghost up here?* I even calculated how fast I could get down the steps if I had to. I was poised now, alert, ready to leap down to the ground if I saw or heard anything.

But I didn't. Everything remained just as it was before he'd run off: the soft, curiously nonbright light all around; the clear trickle of water. I kept trying to see if there was anything moving in the windows of the house. But nothing seemed different to me.

Then I felt exhausted, so much so that I just sat right down at the top of the stairs on the wall and even threw my legs out and stretched out on my back. I looked up. I could make out the constellation of the Archer clearly, just beyond what seemed to be another tall spire of the house. I lay there, smelling the grass and, more distant, ripe honeysuckle, hearing the trickle of water beneath me, and feeling inexplicably calm, as though I were effortlessly floating in cool water on a hot sunny day. Little eddies of air passing over and around me; not a care in the world. I felt as though I could go to sleep. I was so soothed, so comforted.

I don't know how long I rested there. But suddenly it seemed to me that the trickling of the water wasn't just dripping. It had changed somehow, stopping, starting up, modulating slightly—as though someone were sipping from it; as though someone were using its sound to communicate. Softly, very softly but insistently too, as though it had something very important to say, but not in any language I knew, as though someone were trying to talk—a foreigner perhaps, or a woman. I couldn't tell.

Not understanding irritated me then, and I sat up, looked around, and sort of laughed. Here I was, after all of Chas's talk, sitting right up at the Pritchard house on a moonless night, and there was no ghost, no ghost

at all. Grandpa had been right as usual; and Chas…
Then it struck me why Chas hadn't come up to the
house, why he'd done all that talking about not liking
the light and the trickle of water. He'd seen I wasn't
frightened, but he tried to scare me anyway. It was all
an act, because there was no truth at all to his story
about seeing a ghost. None at all.

"You rat!" I said, out loud. "You rotten rat! I'll get you
for that."

A sudden whoosh of wind around the house seemed
to rush at me, half knocking me off my perch. The
water trickled on, babbling, and I was chilled in my little sleeveless polo shirt so that I had to hug myself to
keep from shivering. It seemed to be getting darker
too. Well, I'd been here long enough, no sense in missing my ice cream just to be hanging around here.

I took a final look about me, just so I would be able
to remember it and detail it later, then turned and went
down the steps to the clearing, out of that, and onto the
dirt road. The more I walked, the angrier I became at
Chas for his trying to trick me.

I thought he would be waiting at Atwood Avenue for
me when I got there, and I was all ready with what I
planned to say to him. But he wasn't there. Even angrier, I went across the bridge toward the ice cream store.

It was closed. I couldn't believe it. Closed and shuttered. I walked around to the back of the shop, and it

was closed up there too.

What? Where? I suppose I was really surprised because I went directly to Eileen's house, expecting to find her there. Her mother appeared at the kitchen screen door when I knocked. She held some knitting in her hands and seemed surprised to see me.

"I thought you were with the other children," she said. "They closed a little early tonight. Weren't you with them? Your cousin was."

"No, ma'am," I lied. "I had some chores to do. I thought maybe they were here."

"No. And I don't know where they've gone to. I thought they were at your Grandpa's house."

"Could be," I said. "I wasn't there; I was at a neighbor's, doing my chores," I said, elaborating my lie.

"Oh, well! Then that's where they are. Would you like to come in and have some ice cream? Eileen brought home some blackberry tonight."

"No thanks, ma'am. Ma'am? When did they close tonight?"

"About nine." Then, looking behind her at the kitchen clock set into her oven, she added, "It's almost eleven. I do hope Eileen will be home soon. She's supposed to be in by ten."

"So am I," I said. "Good night. Sorry to bother you."

"If Eileen is still at your Grandpa's, call me. I'll pick her up in the car."

"No bother, ma'am. I'd be happy to walk her home."

"If she isn't… Oh, well. I'm sure everything will be all right. Chas is such a little gentleman."

9

Chas didn't come home for a long time, and he awakened me when he did. I couldn't hear the sound of the television—Mother and Aunt Linda must have turned it off and gone to bed already. Chas didn't put on any lights—I watched him undress in the dull, silver gleam of the moon shining right into one of the bedroom windows.

He must have noticed the moonlight too, because he went over to close the blinds.

"Leave it," I said.

He turned, startled. "I thought you were sleeping."

"A lot of what you thought is phooey."

He decided not to answer that. "It's going to get in my eyes," he said with determination.

"Nothing wrong with a little of your own medicine," I said after he'd left the blinds and settled into his bed.

"What are you talking about?" Chas asked. His voice

sounded not tired, but as though he'd just gotten over some earlier excitement, the way he sometimes sounded late at night telling about some particularly special piece of mischief he'd been involved in.

"You know," I said. I wasn't sure he did. I was simply trying to catch him out.

"How can I?" he asked. Then, "Anyway, I'm tired."

"Running from ghosts?"

He sat up now. I could see his face clearly in the moonlight. Any childlike softness still there was obliterated by the strong coloration. He might have been ten, twenty years older.

"There was something there!" he said. "There was!"

"Oh, yeah. Where? I stayed there so long, I thought I would fall asleep, it was so boring."

"Up on the steps?"

"Yes. And at the well."

"At the well?" He sounded impressed.

"All around the house. I couldn't get in because it was locked shut, even the windows locked. But if I could have, I'm sure it would have been the same—a lot of malarkey."

"I saw something," he insisted.

"What? A ghost?"

"No…but the light was really funny, wasn't it?"

"Not as funny as you thought you were being when you turned around and ran off. Try that trick on Janet or Cathy—they're just kids. Not on me, Chas."

He moved up close to my bed. The moonlight was coming in through the blinds, making sharp pale lines on his head and body.

"I wasn't trying to trick you, Rog."

"To scare me then. You can't tell me you weren't trying to scare me, to make me believe there was something there, when there wasn't."

He seemed to think that over, then he burst out. "Look, Rog. I'll tell you the truth. I lied to you before. I never saw any ghost there. But Rudy Muller did. So when we got there, I remembered what he said, and then, seeing that funny light and hearing that strange watery sound, I got frightened. That's why I ran away. Because I was spooked. Really."

That was exactly what I wanted to hear Chas say. But it had come out too easily—so easily that it sounded wrong now. I knew Chas well enough to know he wouldn't admit to being frightened, especially to me and especially when I hadn't been frightened in the same situation. No, Chas didn't operate like that. Which meant he was telling me what he thought I would believe and hiding something more important: the truth.

"Really, Rog," he said, trying to convince me, uncertain now of my silence.

"Where did you go after you ran out?" I asked.

"Nowhere. I waited a little while at Atwood Avenue, then, when you didn't come out too, I hung around.

"You mean that even though you were so scared for yourself, you would leave me there?"

"You said you weren't scared," he explained.

"You went to Eileen's," I said.

"That's right. I thought you'd meet me there."

"No, you didn't, Chas. You thought that after you ran that I would suddenly get scared too and I would run out too. Only straight home."

Chas didn't say anything then; his face became blank and hard-looking.

"But you weren't planning on going home," I went on. "You were planning all the while on going to Eileen's. When you got there, you told her I couldn't come out or something. You got her to close the store early, and when that was done, you went somewhere with her. That's what her mother told me."

He was silent for a while, thinking up more lies.

"I did trick you, Rog," he said. "But I had a good reason. I wanted to be with Eileen. Alone with her. See, Rog, she really likes me. And I like her too. We wanted to do something together. She promised me we would that night, but we couldn't if you were around. So I had to trick you to be alone with her."

Now I knew Chas was telling the truth. With every word I shrank farther from him. I almost wished I had believed him the first time. I wished now I could stop him from going on.

He didn't. I'd been right to think he was all wound up when he'd come home. Now he let go and talked, all his suppressed excitement from before bursting out of him.

"You know how we talk every night, Rog, how we tell each other all the things we do with girls? All the things we want to do with them. You know how we do them with each other, pretending it's the same thing. Well, that's what I did tonight. Only not pretending. I knew she would let me because she's sweet on me, has been for weeks, for months, really, ever since the summer began, she said, but she was too shy or too stupid or something to say so. Well, yesterday she said she would. We had fooled around a little before, but yesterday she said I could do whatever I wanted. And that's why you would have just been in our way. That's why I had to trick you. Do you see now?"

What Chas said came to me slowly, so slowly, as though it were something I'd heard and was only now remembering. I had to make certain of what he'd said.

"You mean you did what we do…with a girl?"

"Not the same things. Not all of them. But I did some…" and he made a fist with one hand and put the index finger of the other in and out to make certain I knew what he was talking about. "Only in the front."

I was incredulous. "With Eileen?"

"Who else, you jerk! That's who I was with all night."

That hit me worse than anything else he'd said. Knowing Eileen, being so fond of her, thinking of her as so much better than me—certainly miles above Chas—I simply couldn't believe it. At the same time, remembering how she had recently changed her mind about him, how she'd begun saying she'd misunderstood Chas, made me unable to disbelieve him. Even more persuasive was Chas himself, being so proud and offhand. That was the clincher.

"You...you...bastard!" I finally spat out at him. But even this wasn't strong enough, and as I said the word, I punched Chas as hard as I could. He fell off the bed, fell between the two beds, and I jumped down, still shouting, onto his chest and went on punching him blindly, all the while shouting at him. In only a minute he had twisted away from my blows and was on top of me, punching at my face and chest wildly. I grabbed on to his throat and began choking him. He did the same to me. We were there grappling away for only a silent half minute before the bedroom door was thrown open and the light switched on.

"What the hell is going on here?"

It was Grandpa Lynch, in a nightshirt that came down to his knees.

Startled, Chas and I let go of each other's throats.

"Well?" Grandpa demanded. "Get up! What are you two up to, anyway?"

"Nothing, Grandpa," I murmured.

"He went crazy," Chas said, still breathless. "He went crazy and tried to strangle me."

Grandpa looked at Chas, then at me. "When did you get in, Chas? I didn't hear you come in."

Chas hung his head and didn't answer.

"Go back to sleep. The two of you. And if I hear another peep…" He let it hang with an unstated threat. "Go on. Get into your beds. Both of you."

We did, and he shut the light off but left the door ajar when he left.

Chas and I lay in bed with all that still hanging over us. Nothing had been settled. Everything was wrong. I tried to sleep but couldn't. The moon rose higher and higher, shining through the still-open blinds, until it covered the whole opposite wall with a sickly light. I was conscious of Chas also still awake. But I didn't care. I hated him. Hated him and hated Eileen—and hated myself for ever giving a stick for either one of them. They were no good. Chas never had been any good. But now I knew she was just as bad as he was.

After a long time Chas whispered, "I'm sorry, Rog. I didn't know you'd act like this…Rog?"

I didn't answer, and I felt as though I was going to cry. I got up and went out in the hall and crept over to the bathroom. I cried there, muffling my face in a towel; trying not to cry made me do it all the more. I felt so rotten, so betrayed, hating everyone, when all I ever wanted was to be friends with Chas and with Eileen. So many things confused me. I'd never understand why they'd done what they had. Never.

When I finally stepped out of the bathroom, there was some light filtering out of the bottom of Grandpa's study door.

I went and opened it. Grandpa was sitting in his usual chair, reading the Bible. He heard me and looked down the four steps to where I stood sniveling in my underwear.

"Come in. Shut the door," he said gently, as though nothing had happened.

"I'm sorry for waking you up, Grandpa."

"I wasn't sleeping. I hardly sleep anymore. Maybe that's because my body knows its time is running out and supposes it might as well get as much done as possible. But you might have woken your mother and aunt."

I looked at his legs, skinny and mottled, almost brown, sticking out from under the nightshirt. They looked worse than sick people's legs. I hoped Grandpa Lynch wasn't sick too.

"You mustn't swear as you did in there, Roger. Even when you're angry. That was a bad word you used. Do you know what it means?"

"Yes," I answered softly, ashamed of myself.

"Then you mustn't say it again. Come here and kiss me. You didn't before, you know."

I went up and hugged and kissed him. He held me a minute longer than usual, looking into my eyes as though asking me a question, but without words, just by looking.

I wanted so much to talk to him, but I didn't know where to begin or what to say. That sudden gulf opening between us—always so close before—reminded me of my hating Chas and Eileen. I started to cry again.

Grandpa Lynch held me longer, rocking me.

"I don't want to sleep in my room," I whined. "Can I sleep with you?"

"I snore loud as an engine car," he said.

"I don't care."

"You won't be able to come sleep with me for comfort when you grow up, you know. You'll have to face all your troubles and sorrows without your Grandpa's old bones to sleep next to."

"I don't want to grow up," I said, feeling my face turning red. "Not ever."

Grandpa held me so close to him that his mustache scratched my neck, and I could smell pipe tobacco all over his shirt front.

"I'm afraid you won't be able to stop it, boy. I'm afraid you've already begun to grow up tonight," he said softly, as though talking to someone miles and years away.

10

"Well? How does it look? Smaller?" Karen asked.

"Not as small as I thought it would look," I replied. "For all the years I've been away, Nansquett looks remarkably the same."

"I'm glad, darling," she said, nuzzling up against me.

We were seated on the front right fender of my car, parked on Twill Road, right in front of what had once been Grandpa Lynch's house. It didn't look smaller; as a matter of fact, two side wings had been added on, with six extra guest suites, as the big swinging wooden sign on the front lawn announced. It was a vacation motel now, sold by my Aunt Linda and Uncle Al, who'd inherited it more than a decade before, right after Grandpa died. Painted a pale yellow, with dark brown trim on the windows and gables, instead of the ash gray and white it had been. But it was still there, and it brought back whole truckloads of memories, making me happy we had come by here today.

We almost hadn't. I almost didn't turn off the freeway at this exit. But we'd already gone so far out of our way anyway that it didn't make any sense not to stop at Nansquett for a quick look around.

At least that's what Karen said, after I had jokingly suggested we leave the New England Thruway and veer off to the summer community for an hour or two. It would be the last time we'd be this close in years, I hinted. We were on our way back to New York from the Cape. We'd been at Provincetown and Wellfleet for a month—almost all of August, taking our honeymoon, deferred from the year before. Being together so closely the first time for such a long time, we both felt we were still getting to know each other.

What I did know of our sometimes polite, sometimes candid, but always somewhat tentative coming to terms with each other was the quality of our love for each other. Mine had been sudden: The minute I'd walked up to the reference desk of the Forty-Second Street Library and spotted Karen, I know I was in love with her. She was girlish yet businesslike in her mauve corduroy jumper and pale blue frilled-at-the-neck-and-cuffs blouse. I looked at her, waiting my turn on the line. Then, when she asked for my book slip, I handed her one on which I'd written, "I love you. Marry me." Involuntarily her hand had dropped the

slip to the counter and had gone up to her throat, remaining there while she stared at me. Then she recovered enough to ask me if the book was fiction and
who the author was. So I said the same words I'd written, and this time I thought she was going to cry and
shout at me. She'd done neither. She'd gone past me
to the next person in line, an elderly man with a beret
and thick Viennese accent. He was clever enough to
see how smitten I was and, whispering to her, suggested (she later told me) she at least let me buy her
a cup of tea in the nearby restaurant. She did, finally,
unable to get rid of me, and I began a winter-long
siege of her affections, finally succeeding so well, we
were married the following July.

Karen's love for me was based on astonishment.
Lovely as she was, somehow she'd never thought of
herself as being very attractive, never mind marriage-
able. So she had been surprised at first by my over-
whelming desire for her, one that brooked no opposi-
tion; surprised when I later on and more formally
asked her to marry me; surprised when I showed up at
the wedding; surprised when I told her we were to live
in my brownstone duplex; surprised that I didn't walk
out on her, leaving her alone again. Every once in a
while, on our vacation that August, I'd caught her looking at me, as though amazed the marriage had lasted
this long, amazed at herself for being my wife. Amazed

and pleased, because as aggressive and prone to ana-
lyzing and working out everything as I was, she was
just the opposite—cool, instinctual, with an entire set of
intuitive strengths that women are supposed to have
and seldom do: strengths such as knowing that morning as we drove down from the Cape how badly I really did want to see Nansquett, despite my jibing. The
minute I'd brought up the memory I had of the place—
all golden and vague like a late-August afternoon, without a sharp line in the image—she insisted we come
here, if only for the afternoon. Maybe it was the way I
had talked about Grandpa Lynch, or maybe that single
summer I'd spent at Nansquett had made so strong an
impression, it showed through when I spoke of it.

Once we'd veered off the Thruway and onto the
coastal road, I let myself go, telling her more. I de-
scribed the town in detail; I even told her about the
haunted house. I'd awakened a curiosity in her about
my past, and Karen claimed a right to share in that past
because of her interest in the present me.

"Maybe we ought to have come up here instead of
going to the Cape," I suggested. "After all, they have
guest suites."

Karen looked at me quizzically. A month of sun had
covered her with a soft rich tan and brought freckles
that had always been lurking up to the surface. She
hated them. I tried to kiss every one I could find. The

sun had also streaked her heavy ash-blond hair so that it was almost silver-white. She was so beautiful that day, it made my solar plexus itch looking at her. Especially when she saw that I was teasing her. Her face opened up like a tiger lily, and she laughed.

"Next year," she said, "we'll come here. I want to take that room on the far end. There, the one with the checked dimity curtains."

"Ugh. Can't we rethink this?"

"How about over an ice cream soda? Or do you think they still have an ice cream store here?"

I had told Karen about the ice cream store and my first interest, Eileen. I think Karen wanted to see her—grown-up, a mother, fat, with six children.

"Only one way to find out," I said, opening the car door and getting in.

"Sad," Karen said, "how some things change, how they cheapen so quickly." I spun the car into a U-turn back toward Atwood Avenue and the little bridge over the river, and a deep déjà vu set in, so hard and so immediate, I might have been in a trance. Then it settled in with an even harder click, and I had to stop the car.

"What's wrong, Roger?"

"Nothing. I...I just... Yes, this is the spot. The unbroken bushes on the right of the road, the single telephone pole."

"Roger?"

"This is where the haunted house was," I said, not hiding my excitement.

"Here? There's nothing here."

"It's in there. Straight through there. See! Where the trees form an alleyway. That's the dirt road."

Before I could complete the sentence, I had seen it, some twenty feet in and to the left of where I was pointing: a wooden sign, huge red letters on white, that read, FOR SALE: THIS DESIRABLE PROPERTY, 13 ACRES. WHOLE OR DIVIDED INTO LOTS.

"Oh, no! They can't sell it!" I cried.

I jumped out of the car and went up to the sign. Sure enough, it was the Pritchard property. The sign gave a small map of the place. Karen had come up behind me.

"Damn it!" I said. "They'll tear down a perfectly beautiful Victorian mansion and turn it into a trailer park or something."

"Oh, darling," she uttered, hanging on to my shoulder, "Oh, Roger, I'm so sorry." I knew she meant it. Unlike most young women I'd met, Karen genuinely appreciated beautiful old things.

We recrossed the street and were getting into the car when I said, "Look! Why don't we go take a look at it? It's the last time we can."

She got out of her side and came around to kiss me. "I'd love to see your old haunted house."

We pushed over the bushes and brambles and, hand

in hand, entered the long sun-splattered alley of trees. They were more overgrown than I recalled, and there were many more dead leaves and branches on them than I remembered too: molding clumps of leaves surrounded their lower trunks; wan white little mushrooms grew one third of the way up even the tallest of the trees. We were instantly inside another kind of day from the hot striking summer outside on the road: a dark, loamy day, rich with bittersweet decay. The light seemed utterly different too, as though the aging and rotting forest around us had permeated it completely with tiny chips of matter that hung in the air, making colors and shapes bend and change. We walked through the alleyway of tall old trees like children lost in the woods in some Grimm's fairy tale.

"This is where we turn," I said, half whispering.

It was less dark here. Many trees had fallen across the dirt road, felled by decrepitude or winter storms. We had to pick our way over them carefully.

"Look, wagon tracks" Karen pointed out.

"I don't think an automobile ever came up this road," I said.

"Really! Oh, Roger..." But she didn't go on.

When we reached the end of the trees, the road opened out just as I recalled it, but larger than I remembered (at night all distances seem smaller).

"Oh!" she said with a little gasp. She stood blinking

with the most curious expression on her face.

"What?" I asked, following her eyes around the little area, past the ground-level stable doors set into a sloping ground, over to the long fieldstone wall with its two flights of stone steps that almost but never quite met as they rose, and on to the curved turret of the house, barely visible from where we stood. Ivy covered the wall's surface, except on the steps, which were mossy and where the water from the broken well trickled down, winding through the large flat stones, making a shiny wet path down to a tiny deep puddle on the ground.

"Well?" I asked.

"It's wonderful!" Karen said, at the same time furrowing her brows, as she did whenever she was about to break into some minor disagreement with me. "Really, Roger. Wonderful."

"Let's go up and look at the house." I pulled her along and then put her in front of me, going up the treacherous-looking steps. All the while I talked. "There wasn't really any ghost here, although everyone said so in the town. I disproved that theory for myself—brave, stupid little twelve-year-old stubborn kid that I was at the time. Of course, I'd never been in the house. It was all shut up and locked. But, look! There's the well. Half tumbling over. What, Karen? What is it?"

She had stopped at the top of the stairs and looked

around, clutching her arms to her chest, as though shivering. "I don't know," she said, looking straight at me, and her confused look confirmed that. "I don't know. Maybe you talked about it so much that it...looks so...well, familiar!"

"Familiar?"

"Not that I've ever been here or even really seen the place. But, yes, familiar. And wonderful too! It feels so nice just being here, standing here. Oh, Roger, look. The house isn't shut and locked. Do you think we could go in?"

A dim idea was beginning to form in my mind, just below the surface of my consciousness. I didn't know for sure what it was, but I did know that if I let it come, it would. Karen's pleasure in the place made me want the idea to rise up, to become a real thought. Going into the house could only help it along, helping further to congeal the tenuous idea.

One of the double front doors was off its hinge, inviting us, so we stepped over it and in.

"It's huge!" she said.

The foyer was immense and opened up to large rooms on either side. But it was dominated by a long, curved staircase ascending to a balcony, which gave onto two sets of rooms, two or three doorways on either side of the landing. Light filtered down through a centrally placed stained-glass window above the staircase, acting like a skylight, bathing the foyer in sheets of wine and honey and lime colors. Even with all the dust and cobwebs that draped room after room and the cluttered furniture stacked over itself and covered with drop cloths, the place seemed inviting and comfortable.

"It's really magnificent," I said after we'd done a fast circuit of the downstairs rooms.

"Magnificent," she echoed, as breathless as I was.

Still hand in hand, we slowly wandered through the first floor again, from a large music room with scroll-work ornaments on its walls and ceiling, to a breakfast room, up a set of stairs from the parlor corridor, looking over the front of the house, to more parlors and dining rooms, back to the foyer.

"Let's go up," Karen said. I knew how she felt. I had to see what the upstairs looked like too.

"There may be a ghost," I warned jokingly.

"Who cares! It'll just have to move out…or somehow adjust to us."

"You mean…?" I realized that was the idea that had been forming.

"I don't know what I mean," she said. "Let's go up-stairs."

There were three large rooms on one side of the house, connected to each other by four small chambers that must have been dressing rooms. Two more large bedrooms and another two smaller ones were on the other side. There was also a stairway leading farther up. "To the tower," I said.

"Off with his head!" she said, leading me up.

I stopped her on the stairway and hugged her.

"You know I'd do anything in the world you want, Karen. Anything!"

As usual, whenever I made this kind of gesture, she was both touched and embarrassed.

"To the tower!" she repeated.

Like all the other rooms, this one was untouched except for age and dust and spiders' work. Still, I wasn't prepared for it.

"Why, it's a study!"

"Hardly a study," she corrected me. "It's a real honest-to-God library. Look, Rog. Shelving up to the ceiling. It looks like it's mahogany, trimmed with teak."

Twenty feet in height and diameter, the library was a huge six-sided room, drenched in light from its own multifaceted hexagonal skylight, every pane of the yellowed glass intact. Shelves filled with sets of books lined each wall but one. On that one, halfway up, a wooden staircase rose to a small cast-iron balcony ten feet high. Up there were four high windows, each with its own recessed window seat.

Before I could say how familiar this looked to me, Karen had climbed the little stairway and managed to open one of the windows.

"You won't believe this, Roger."

I was at her side, on the windowsill in a second.

"You can see for miles, Roger. For miles!"

It was true. From this window we could see to the river, along its length down to the spit of land containing the shore houses along Twill Road. We went to the next window, opened it, and saw the entire front part of the house, along Atwood Avenue, right to the courthouse office. From a third window we could look north, far past the restored mill, right to the highest roofs of Scituate. We stood and leaned, looking for a long time, then went downstairs quietly and began to inspect the book bindings, afraid to touch them for fear they might crack and disintegrate under our touch. Then we went down to the bedroom and, still silent, down to the first floor. Without looking back, we stepped over the awry door and out onto the lawn.

Karen spun around then, looking back at the house, and again I could see her brows knit. Then she spoke: "We can't. We just can't!"

"Can't what?" I asked.

"We can't let them tear it down and make a ranch development out of it. We can't, Roger. You know we can't. Not now that we've seen it."

"We won't then. We'll buy it."

"All of it?"

"The whole damn thing. All thirteen acres. We'll buy

it and restore it and come stay here in the summer."

"It'll cost," she warned. "Money and time."

"Do you care?" I asked. I didn't care about either the money or the time. I had both in abundance.

Karen didn't answer, but her look said no, that she'd pay any price, no matter how high.

With the decision formed, we became suddenly serious, grave, silent as we walked back to the car. I stopped at the sign to see who the real estate agent was. It simply read, COUNTY ASSESSOR'S OFFICE. COURTHOUSE BUILDING.

The county assessor turned out to be the justice of the peace and the local sheriff: a little, balding middle-aged Italian-American with an operatic face and a bulbous nose.

"It's been sold to the county," he said. "That's why we're the ones handling it."

"How much is it?" I asked.

"It's thirteen acres, you know. Within five minutes' walk to the beach. A large place. 'Course there's an old house there too. But that can be taken down easily. Know of some folks in Scituate who'd do it for you cheap."

"How much is it," I repeated, "as it is?"

He stopped the sales talk then and looked at me. "You folks from Providence?"

"New York. But I'm not going to develop the land, if

that's what you're really asking. I want to keep it in one piece and restore the Pritchard house."

"How do you know it's called that?"

"I just know."

"Well, mister," there was a pause, "a big contractor from Fall River came over here just a few days ago, looking at it. What did you say your name was?"

"Lynch. Roger Lynch."

That stopped him. "Any relationship to Ralph Lynch?"

"He was my grandfather."

He smiled. "The finest man I ever knew."

"Even better than that!" I put in.

"You want to live up there?" he asked, unsure.

"Ever since I was a boy here," I said. "I can't live in Grandpa's house."

"No. No. That's too bad." He shook his head and looked down at the papers in his hand. "You know, Mr. Lynch, there are some people in this town who want it all to become like your grandpa's place—guest motels and hamburger stands. But I don't."

"Then help me to stop it," I said. "Sell the place to me instead of the builders from Fall River."

"You're almost a native too," he said, as though looking for further reasons. "You'll live up here?"

"In the summers. Once it's all fixed up."

"That's going to cost."

"We can't live in it as it is."

"No. You're right." He pulled the sheaf of papers out of a file and showed me the figures. "This was what the town paid the Todd heirs for the Pritchard property. This is what those people from Fall River quoted."

"I can't match that," I said sincerely. "But I can give you double what the town paid the Todds for it. And I can give the town back its past too."

"Sign here! It isn't final, mind. But it'll keep it out of those vultures' hands until we can make the proper arrangements."

I signed all the copies he shoved in front of me, then shook hands with him. He was smiling all over now, glad he had done it.

"And a Lynch too. Wait until Mama B. hears about this. They'll be two of you Lynches in town now. Young and full of energy. Just like in the old days."

"Two of us? How?"

"Chas Lynch. He still lives here, even though his mother died last year. He rents out one part of their house to another family."

"Chas!" I said. "He's my cousin," I told Karen. "God, I wonder if he's anything the way he used to be."

She stared at me. Later on she told me she'd never heard me speak like that about anyone, vague as I was. We had stepped out of the office and were standing on the courthouse steps.

"And behind there," I said, pointing to the other side of the building, "is where the town library is. I used to come here twice, three times a week. So, you see, you weren't the first librarian I was sweet on. C'mon. Let's go take a look."

"Can't!" the assessor said. "It's closed. Been closed for more than two years. We can't seem to find a librarian willing to live in a town like this. The last one came from Scituate. Then she moved up to Pawtucket, when her husband got a job there."

The look that passed between Karen and me could have knocked a truck off the highway.

"Darling," I began tentatively, "you don't think…?"

Her hand went up to her mouth, her agate eyes almost glittering with surprise and pleasure at me.

"I think you may have found yourself a new librarian" I told the assessor.

"Part-time," she put in.

"Hell! That's better than nothing. Let me see if I can get the keys. I'll show it to you."

We went back to his office for the keys. It was only then that I noticed his name on the door: Harold Bianchi. Could he be Bud Bianchi? The kid who used to help Eileen's mother?

I was almost afraid to ask. When I did, he responded with a laugh and another ten minutes of gossip about all of the folks I still remembered from the town.

"Hell!" he said finally. "I haven't had a talk like that in years. You see! I was right to let you have it."

11

The plumbers and electricians and carpenters had been coming and going every day for the past four months—so I naturally assumed it was one of them returning for a last-minute consultation or piece of unfinished work when I heard the car pull into the driveway late that hazy spring afternoon.

Although I was in the upstairs turret library, close to a window giving a view of the area, I didn't bother looking out to make certain. I was too immersed in my work, replacing sets of the old books into the newly polished mahogany shelving on the little balcony. I was following the plan that Karen and I had worked out a few weeks before, when we'd finally gotten all the volumes catalogued. Another morning's work, and the library would be complete, restored to exactly the condition it had been in a hundred years before, save for such contemporary modifications as electric lighting, a telephone extension cord, and auxiliary speakers wired to the huge system two floors down in the music room. But these were barely noticeable when the room was seen. The library had been one of the most remarkable rooms in the place, a key to our deciding to take the house. There was a sense of real accomplishment in its being almost done, which made up for the enormous expense and the multitude of problems we'd run into during the restoration.

Downstairs the kitchen, the breakfast room, the little connecting parlor, the music room, and the immense foyer were restored. The north side was still awaiting work. On the second floor only the two rooms beneath the library had been completed—a wall taken out to make them into one huge bedroom with a dozen windows, and the two dressing rooms combined into a modern bath and dressing room. The other three rooms on the north side remained empty, awaiting their turn. The house was so large, another family could have been living on the other side of the foyer and we'd only know about it by bumping into them coming or going, especially since the clever architect of the past century saw to it that several alternate staircases had been provided for—little twisting ones that opened up from what you might have thought was only another of many closets and went up to another dressing room or down to another part of the vast basement.

After dinner and whatever final night work we had to do, Karen and I would wander around the house. Down into the basement with flashlights and extension cords to find all the furniture that still hadn't been re-stored—destined when done for the north side of the house. It sat dusted and brushed of cobwebs but still rather sad and dilapidated compared to what had al-ready been repaired and polished to a high gleam with oils of clove and lemon and which now elegantly graced the furnished rooms. Or Karen and I would go to the north side of the house, sketchpads in hand, planning out various designs for how we would even-tually fix up those rooms—for guests or children.

Often enough our wandering led us outside on balmy nights, or, when curtailed by weather or sheer fatigue or merely the need to be close together for a while, we'd jump into the big four-poster bed we'd found on the north side of the house, complete with various side curtains and half-dozen drawers of various sizes (and functions?), built in to the headboard and footboard. There we'd feel as though we'd stepped back into another time, and we'd approach each other with a cautious affection and reserved passion or sim-ply lie in each others arms, me talking about almost anything, Karen occasionally commenting or often merely listening. Most of the time we would go right to sleep, exhausted. We worked awfully hard at the house, even with the half-dozen workmen always there, hammering or sawing or drilling away day after day. Besides working on the house, Karen had managed to get the library opened again and was now there five days a week from noon until six in the evening, making that part of the town's past alive again. Although we'd thought we would remain in New York and only come up here summers, as soon as we'd obtained the house in late fall, we'd come up and begun working, and it was an unspoken agreement that we would continue living here, letting out my town house next year. And being at the house all winter and seeing the spring arrive, we knew it had been exactly the right thing. We'd gotten so much done already.

But handsome as the downstairs rooms were, the library in the turret was our real accomplishment. Especially once we'd discovered the books were in startlingly fine condition despite their age. Perhaps they'd been sealed off somehow, or neglect had been the best thing for them. No one and nothing had touched them for almost a century; no unfiltered sunlight had entered in to heat and dry and crack them; no rain or moisture had gotten through the heavily insulated wainscoting to eat them away by mold. Cataloguing them, seeing what they were, had been a joy for us—Karen had been high on it for weeks. Many, naturally, were of no value, except for their age. But many others

seemed to be rare even for their own time. Sets of
Voltaire, Hegel, and Plato in Greek and Latin sat alongside sets of Samuel Richardson, Smollett, Marivaux,
and Fielding. But there were rarities too—an early
translation into English of some Buddhist texts, a surprising set of Kierkegaard's works in German. And with
all this, children's albums the Pritchards had put together as well as scores of bound volumes of the Reverend Calvin Pritchard's tedious and tendentious trea-
tises on the relationship of Man to his Providence and
vise versa, ad nauseum.

Amity had inherited this semiliterary bent from her
father, as another dozen vellum-bound volumes testi-
fied. I had laid these aside on the long oblong distressed-oak reading table in the center of the room and
would occasionally skim through them at random
when I needed a break: a cup of coffee, a cigarette, a
little Brahms piano music.

Unsurprisingly, these attempts of hers were childish
self-criticisms aimed at self-improvement—more than
likely written under the Reverend's example, if not actually under his eye. But the fact that they were hers
made them fascinating to me. For I was living in her
house, almost as it had been when she had lived in it,
sitting here in the same room where she had written
them, reading her words.

They absorbed me, as the library absorbed me, as

the restoration of the house absorbed me—so that I was living in a state of suppressed excitement, of pleasure and anticipation of some discovery, and with a deeply increasing sense of how the past could be made part of the present—integral to it, if done with involvement and affection.

It was this absorption that kept me from noticing him in the open library doorway, from even hearing him climb the second-floor stairs to get up here, that kept me from seeing he was standing there looking at me for some time: He had to cough loudly to get my attention.

"I'd heard you'd come back to Nansquett. But I wouldn't believe it until I laid eyes on you for myself."

His voice was loud and deep in the reverberant room. I turned around looking for its source before I thought to look at the doorway. And then I faced him for a minute or so trying to snap back out of my day-dreams about Amity and her time into the practical now. He wore a work shirt, jeans and mud-caked construction boots. My first impression was on a new man contracted to do something in the house, reporting for instructions. Then I thought perhaps this is someone who knew me from my visits to the town with my family and had come to say hello.

"I'd heard that my little cousin Roger had come back to Nansquett, rich as Rockefeller and crazy as a coot. But I had to see for myself."

Now the figure of the man melted into a memory—yes! The same curly blond hair, darker now; the same fine facial features, covered with grime and a blond fuzz on his cheeks and chin; but especially the same mocking smile and the still astonishingly dark eyes.

"Chas?"

"Who the hell else? Amity Pritchard?" He laughed now. "C'mon down off there and greet me like I'm a white man."

Marveling at how little he'd changed, I descended from the balcony and went to shake his hand. He'd grown. He was two or three inches taller than me, large, solid, muscular.

"Shit!" he said, scorning my extended hand and pulling me into a crushing embrace. He hugged me once or twice, murmuring something unintelligible, until I pulled away, trying to make a joke of it.

"Well, you haven't changed," I kidded him. "Still a ninety-pound weakling."

He ignored that, saying "No, I haven't changed. But you have. No more baby fat. You're all trimmed down. Looking good. Looking younger than you ought to too. I guess it's all that rich living."

"I swim," I said by way of explanation. "Ever since high school, I've been swimming." The way his eyes were smoking at me from their deep sockets made me think he wanted something from me. And his reference to how rich I was suggested he would soon be hitting me up for a loan. I nerved myself for dealing with it.

"I know I should have gotten in touch with you, Chas," I said in an attempt to forestall any such accusations from him, "but we've really been a little driven getting all this into shape."

He frowned a little at that, then looked around at the library.

"Well, you're doing quite a job here. Quite a job! People in town are talking about it already. Wait until you're done. It'll really set them going." He walked around the room a little, looking up and down, as though admiring details. "Jesus, I never knew this place was so big and so, well, so big!"

"It's a beautiful house, Chas. Really beautiful. As good as anything in Newport."

He continued looking around, then suddenly turned to me. "I thought maybe you didn't choose to look me up because, well, because you were still sore with me."

"Sore?"

"You know. The last time we saw each other wasn't under the most favorable circumstances."

I felt the blood rush to my face. I tried making light of it. "We were just kids then, Chas."

"I know. I know. But some people don't forget anything. That's why I didn't come here sooner, even though I've known since last November that you were living here. Bud Bianchi told me as soon as your papers came through." He went to the table and began looking at the volumes of Amity's diaries, fingering their pages. My first instinct was to ask him to leave them alone.

"And I wouldn't have come here today if your wife hadn't told me I'd better."

"Karen?"

"At the library," Chas said. "I went there to get a book on electronics. That's my hobby: electronics. Radios and televisions. I'm taking courses for it in a night school in Cranston two nights a week. Right now I'm an automobile mechanic. Partners in a big garage and triple gas pump up in Scituate. You ever have any problems with your car, bring it up to us. I'll give you a discount."

"Thanks, Chas."

"Yeah, well, I knew she was your wife, everyone in town knows that much. And as I was checking out this book on electronics, I said, 'Tell Roger his cousin Chas sends his regards.' She took me aside and sort of yelled at me for not coming to see you. She said you'd mentioned me fondly at times and that by all rights you ought to have looked me up but that you were so busy up here that you didn't have any time to go visiting. Well, I have plenty of time even with the garage and the night courses. So I came."

"Well, Karen was right. As usual."

He dropped the diary. "She's a beautiful woman, Roger. Certainly the best-looking woman in this town for years."

"Thanks, Chas."

He looked as though he wanted to say more, but he was silent for a minute until he finally said, "You are still sore."

This was where the hit for the loan came. "Not at all."

"Well, then why are you so goddamn distant?"

That was a new one.

"That was years ago, Roger," Chas continued. "Unimportant too. Just a goddamned little girl. Unimportant, Roger. You and I had something far more important. We were friends. You were the only close good friend I ever had. The only friend I ever cared for. You shouldn't have let a girl get in our way. You should have known better than that."

"Who even remembers," I said, trying to change the subject.

"*I* remember. We were close, goddamn it. You can't just stand there and say it isn't so."

"We were kids then, Chas."

"We were goddamn lovers!" he said, spitting the words out in my face and at the same time dropping his hands to his sides and turning away. "Kids or not. And for that I deserve more than years of silence, then six

months of your cold shoulder. It's humiliating. I know
I wasn't the best kid in the world, Roger, but I never
did anything half this cruel to you. That last week at
Grandpa's house, and now—now that you've come
back. Why did you come back anyway?" he demanded.

"I don't know. We were passing through. We saw the
sign about the house being for sale. We came up and
looked at the house. I don't know, Chas."

He was restless again. He'd go off to one wall of the
room, touch a binding or detail of shelving, then come
back to me as though magnetically drawn.

"So that's it?" he asked, almost out of nowhere.

"What's it?"

"Hello, cousin. Good-bye. Good luck."

"Well, what else? Do you want to stay for dinner. I'll
ring Karen and tell her you're staying."

He laughed mirthlessly. "No, I don't want to stay for
dinner."

"Well, what then? I don't know."

"You saw this house then, when we were kids, isn't
that right? And that's why you came back."

"More or less right," I admitted.

"I'll tell you what I want, Roger. I want us to be
friends again, the way we used to be."

"Well, we have to start somewhere then. Come by for
dinner tonight, and—"

"That's not what I meant. I mean I want us to spend

time together, Roger, like we used to do. Afternoons. When your wife is at work and I have time off."

It was the tone of his voice more than the words he was using that warned me he was asking for something not conveyed.

"All right. But I'll have to have time too, Chas. After all, until I'm done with this restoration—"

He interrupted me again. "You'll find time if you want to."

Now I knew I couldn't sidestep anymore. "To do what, Chas? To get together afternoons and do what? Have you talk to me about repairing Buicks and me talk to you about Hegel? Is that what you want?"

"No. Not to talk. To do what we used to do—remember, at night, up at Grandpa's house?"

"I'm married," I said.

"So what? What I'm talking about has nothing to do with being married."

"It has everything to do with it."

"And besides, you were mine first," he said. "I still have the first claim on you."

"Chas, you've got to be joking. I haven't done anything like that in years."

"You'll remember. You learned fast enough."

"It's different now, Chas. We didn't know what we were doing then. We do now. It isn't right. It's just not natural."

He flared up again, pinned me against the table.

"Don't give me that shit. It's just as natural as anything else. All love is sick, Roger, whether between a man and a woman or a man and anything. Believe me, I've seen it, I know it. I don't have any degrees in philosophy from fancy colleges, but I've got eyes and ears. I've seen, and I know. I know I've never felt the same way about anyone else but you, and I know it's the same with you. That's why you came back to Nansquett. I knew you would. I didn't know when, but I knew it would be sometime. When I came here and stood in this doorway watching you, I was sure of it. We're bound up, Roger, bound up, and we'd better roll with it, otherwise it's going to really get bad for us."

"You'd better let go of me now, Chas," I said coldly, calmly, trying to hide the fear that I felt, a real fear worse than any I'd known in my life because it was so indistinct.

He released my arms and stood back.

"C'mon, Rog. Just once. For old time's sake. Let me show you. C'mon, Rog."

It was the way he had whispered to me that first night in Grandpa Lynch's house, panting, desirous, manipulative as an Eighth Avenue prostitute. I hadn't known then where it would lead to, what passions would explode in me, what would be revealed to me about myself. I did now.

"I can't, Chas."

"What you mean is, you won't."

"I can't, Chas. I've got a wife now. I love her. I don't love you like her, Chas. I'm sorry. And I'm sorry that you've never found someone to love in a mature way. But you will, Chas, if you get rid of these childish ideas and start acting like a grown-up."

He was silent, waiting for me to finish my lecture. Then he was still and silent, cold and white-faced with anger and humiliation.

"Suit yourself," he said in a toneless, small voice.

His saying those words, in that same tone of voice he'd used so long ago, disturbed me even more than his declaration of his continued passion for me, disturbed me with possibilities of remembered mischiefs, for past slights he'd been so bent on achieving.

"Chas," I tried. "Listen. Stay over for dinner, and we'll talk about it later. You'll see that—"

"Suit yourself," he repeated and left the room, running down the stairs so fast, he was halfway down the next landing to the first floor before I even reached the hallway.

I remained where I was, stunned, until I heard the front door slam open and shut, then heard the car engine start up, the engine being gunned and the tires squealing out of the dirt road. Then I turned and went to the work table and lifted a volume of Amity's diary and waited until I could no longer hear the sound of his car engine.

I lit a cigarette then, listening to the first tentative splatter of raindrops tapping on the stained-glass skylight, opened the diary, and began to read.

12

I had picked up the volume at random, picked it up and held it to my chest to protect myself, to defend myself from Chas and from the past he so much wanted to continue into the present. When I finally opened it to read, it was with the intent of banishing the troubling present he represented by immersing myself in the past—Amity's past—no matter how banal. I couldn't have know how crucial that act would be for me, for Chas, for Karen—for Amity too.

At first I read blindly, without making a great deal of sense of anything: Each entry in that florid but correct handwriting of hers detailed the minutiae of the life of a spinster more than a hundred years before—how she had made soap from fat drippings strained through cheesecloth to clean out impurities and mixed with spoonfuls of lye; how she had prepared possets to cure her father's sore throat with potent

mixtures of lemons and honey boiled with cloves;
how she was beginning to teach her Negro servants
how to sew complicated stitches so they might ply
their needles for profit; and how to cook without
using heavy lard, which often caused sensitive stom-
achs indigestion. I read of quiet evenings of knitting
and small talk in back parlors; of insignificant gossip
about people in Nansquett and Scituate now long
dead. I perused her neatly divided columns of tabula-
tions of money spent on items bought in the town and
of wages paid out to the servants and local trades-
people. I read her reflections about the relation of a
religious man or woman to an all-ruling Deity. For
page after page, these words from another time swam
before my eyes, as I sought and finally managed to
achieve forgetfulness of what had just happened in
the library between Chas and me.

I was about to close this volume of Amity's diary, to
go get myself an afternoon snack, when one entry
struck me:

August 26, 1866: This morning I had the good
fortune of making a new acquaintance: Captain
Eugene V. Calder of the Union Army. He came to
visit today, following delivery of my dear Alfred's
last letter yesterday afternoon by the hand of
young Ted Wilcomb. We spoke of Alfred for al-

most two hours, reviving in my mind and soul all that I lost when that dear man, my affianced, was felled in battle last year at the Manassas.

Two days later was another intriguing entry:

August 28, 1866: Captain Calder called on me again today. We sat in the music room. He is a most intelligent and courteous man. We spoke of Alfred again. Captain Calder has a multitude of anecdotes about my departed fiancé, as they were close friends throughout the course of the past conflict.

He remains with the Wilcombs for a few weeks more, lightening Ameilia Wilcomb's burden by being for a while the son she lost by the hand of a divine fate.

He has asked if he might call on me again. I said he might.

From then on there was an entry almost every day:

August 29, 1866: Captain Calder played the piano today. I know so few men who are not profes-sional musicians who have any ability at that in-strument. He is most accomplished in all respects. I fully understand my Alfred's admiration for him.

August 30, 1866: Captain Calder came for our afternoon Sunday dinner. I do not think Constance likes him as well as I do. He teased her lightly about her constant reference to her beaux. She became quite flushed and later on told me she believed he was quite overbearing.

August 31, 1866: I consented to drive with Captain Calder today. He is a careful and expert driver. He declared that Alfred Wilcomb, whom he always thought the most intelligent of men, was a fool not to have married me before he went off to war. I was startled to hear this and showed my disapproval. He later apologized for his effusiveness.

September 2, 1866: Eugene stayed for dinner this evening. Later, we played a game of cards—the first in this house—although without any stakes, so it cannot be construed as gambling in any sense. As in all else he does, Eugene Calder is both expert and expert in teaching others. I learned several strategies from him, and they very much amazed me when they worked: I especially enjoyed *bluffing* Constance, who was very irritated to later on discover I did not at all hold the cards she thought (and I intimated) I held, thereby winning the tricks over her.

Catulla, Saturn's old wife, later on told me she had never before seen such a fine man as the Captain. He is handsome; although as a rule I do not prefer fair men. Alfred was as dark-skinned as an Italian or Spaniard, although of good blood. Eugene's hair and mustachios are a fine, silky blond. His eyes are almost golden, they are such a light yet fiery brown.

September 5, 1866: Eugene for dinner again. I played two of Mr. Mendelssohn's "Songs Without Words" at the piano; and Eugene was so smitten with one, he asked me to play it again and again. It has become my favorite piece of music. Once Constance's beau came for her, Eugene pressed my hand to his lips and told me he will not leave Nansquett for another two weeks. His eyes were bright with desire and longing. I was glad when Constance's beau came in looking for her soda mints; for otherwise, I would have been unable to break away from Eugene's hold.

September 9, 1866: He can no longer remain with the Wilcombs. Catulla has prepared a room for him under father's library—next to father's old bedroom. Our own rooms are far enough away to be considered almost another dwelling.

September 11, 1866: Constance has parted from
her beau. She cried for almost an hour. I tried to
comfort her, but to no avail. How can I share in
her distress when I am happier day after day being
with E?

September 15, 1866: He has asked me to be his
wife. We were in the formal parlor, not much used
since our mother and father passed on. I asked
whether Eugene were proposing to me merely out
of an obligation to his friendship for Alfred. He
persuaded me this was not so but said he thought
that Alfred would have given his fullest blessing
upon our undertaking if I could be persuaded
that Alfred were hovering overhead, our guardian
angel. I have asked for a week to give Eugene my
answer.

September 19, 1866: I do not think Constance ap-
proves of our proposed marriage. When I told her,
she began to pout. Today, while Eugene was out
with Saturn inspecting the harvest of Concord
grapes in the little ravine, Constance and I spoke
of Eugene. I believe she feels compromised in
some way by his residing with us in the same
house. I tried to allay her fears—with little success,
I fear.

September 20, 1866: I have accepted Eugene's hand. After dinner tonight we went into the music room—the hallowed place where we first discovered the secret affections in each others hearts!—and Eugene once again made his proposal although a week has not fully passed from his earlier declaration. When I said I would accept, he rose from his knees and kissed me quite passionately upon my lips. It was only with a great effort of will that I could persuade him to find another seat while we talked of our upcoming nuptials, he wished to be so close to me.

September 21, 1866: Eugene has written to his mother in Vermont, narrating our plans for marriage. He also asks for her consent.

September 23, 1866: Has a woman ever so loved a man? I cannot think it. I allowed Eugene to kiss me again tonight. But I was once more forced to persuade him aside. He is a passionate man, filled with the vigor and virility of his gender. This causes many little happy difficulties in our friendship. Yet I know that he is guided in all this by the unswerving hand of love, and I cannot blame him. Fires also seize my limbs when we are alone together.

The courtship continued for almost another month. Managerial duties and home recipes—not to mention religious and even philosophical musings—gave way to her daily intimately increased fascination with Calder. Then there came a curious entry, quite different in tone from any previous:

October 16, 1866: May Father forgive me! May God have compassion on the wanderings of a storm-tossed and weakened woman!

Today Eugene received a missive from his mother. She consents to our marriage, with the simple stipulation that E. return to Vermont for a short time to secure all of his and the family's affairs, as we plan to live here in Nansquett. He plans to leave me in two days' time.

This afternoon Eugene once again demanded a pledge from me to ensure that I will await him. I still do not understand why my word is not good enough for him: He uses it to swear upon all sorts things and in all sorts of situations. Under much duress I gave him his required pledge—my precious maidenhood. Here in this very library, where Father was wont to daily come and have deep and spiritual intercourse with higher thoughts, did Eugene and I... I cannot say it. I cannot write one word more.

One more entry dated the 18th of October notes that the Captain had left for Vermont. Amity was disturbed that he had demanded further pledges from her—one every day he remained under her roof. In all the moralizing and distress, she also expressed her terror of the passionate feelings Calder had aroused in her: feelings equal if not greater than his own.

For the following two months, her diary entries returned to their previous domestic and ethical concerns. Then another startling one appears:

December 29, 1866: There is no doubt about it: I am with child. Catulla has assisted at many birthings among the servants; she confirmed the still unglaring fact with great joy. However, I can feel no pleasure in this unexpected result of my conjunction out of the sacraments of matrimony: only foreboding. And only two letter from Eugene since he went away. Both of them only serving to extend his delay—now he will not be back in Nansquett until spring! Ought I write him my news? Catulla says certainly, as he is the father. But I do not know how he will take the news. With joy; for if not I could not bear to live with myself. Ought I tell Constance? Do I dare? I no longer know who I can trust and who not. I cannot go visiting for succor, as I am inquired of by all when will Eugene

return and when will the banns be posted. It is
most distressing.

From then on followed an increasingly frightened series of entries, each one detailing Amity's growing
shame, her sadness, her uncertainty of her worth in
Calder's eyes should he find out her pregnancy. And
with it all, her growing alienation from her friends, her
neighbors, his sister—once so confided in. Christmas
and New Year's come and go. Constance's spirits are at
their highest, although Amity does not know why. Then
she discovers that Eugene has been in communication
with Constance. Unlike her own letters from him, those
to Constance are playful and very tender. Amity re-
solves to write to Eugene about the child. The return
letter from him ignores her pregnancy and once more
delays his return. Amity's depression and isolation in-
crease. She begins to complain of migraine headaches.
She dismisses servants who have been with the
Pritchards for years, based on mere misdemeanors.
Constance avoids her. Then, on Easter Sunday there is
the following entry:

April 18, 1867: I can no longer be seen without my
condition being immediately remarked upon. I
have taken to my room and put out the rumor
through Constance that I have taken a bad ague

which requires bed rest. Constance is very kind
and understanding. How I lover her. How I mis-
takenly failed to trust her before. She will do all
she can to protect me.

Very few entries deal with her condition, until June
10, when the next poignant entry reflects the resolu-
tions of her problem:

June 10, 1867: The child was born dead yesterday
afternoon. I had Saturn bury it somewhere off the
end of the property. I do not know where, and because it was unbaptized, there is no need for a
marker. I am still not well. The labor was long and
very painful. Constance was by my side for hours.
She is my only remaining strength. She has been
at my bedside all morning, cheering me up by
reading a new novel she had sent especially for me
from Boston, by Mrs. Gaskell. I could not concentrate on her words, with all of my own terrifying
thoughts, and she must perforce reread to me the
entire opening all over again.

The child was born a month too early. God has
seen fit to punish me for my lust and greed in
wishing to possess the body of…I cannot write his
name. Tonight, Constance will write to him in my
name to tell him of the disastrous news.

There are a few more minor entries—then two months of silence. When the diary picks up again, it is with this entry:

July 21, 1867: Eugene returns tomorrow. I have his last letter in my hand as I write this. I cannot believe what he writes. He thinks we ought not have hurried so into a decision of marriage. We were blinded by our great common affection for our departed Alfred, he writes. He wishes us to reconsider our plans. Dear Lord, that I should have suffered so in pains of childbearing for this!

When I showed this letter to Constance, she merely laughed at me. "Are you amazed?" she asked, the vixen. "What man wants a wife of such easy virtue." God help me, but I struck her face for those words. I later repented and asked for forgiveness. But she walked away and has kept to her room.

The diary goes blank for another two weeks, then:

August 4, 1867: Eugene and Constance were married two days past at my Aunt Raines Todd's house in Bristol. They return tomorrow. This last month has been an inferno for me. They have been together in the house all this week, doing I cannot

say what, as I never saw them. Eugene never came
to my room. Constance will still not accept my
apologies.

This is God's judgment on me for my lust and
anger and wickedness. May I now learn to accept
my fate with humility.

Amity tried. Upon the newlyweds' return to Nansquett, she greeted them warmly, with the servants all
gathered in the formal parlor to toast them with cham-
pagne. She later presided over an extravagant wedding
dinner, at which a few of her Todd relatives and two of
the Wilcombs were in attendance. Outwardly, at least,
she seemed to accept the horrifying situation of their
entanglement. Inwardly, her torments raged on. As the
months went by and Calder and Constance settled into
the house, Amity moved to her father's bedroom under
the library turret on the south side of the house, leaving the north side for them. Instead of improving, however, their situation worsened. By the following summer, there were few entries in her diary. All the more
of a surprise then to encounter this one:

June 18, 1868: Today, while inspecting the servants' cleaning of the Calder suite of rooms, I
came upon Eugene shaving at his bureau. He
wore no shirt or undergarment, and his trousers

hung almost off his hips. He spotted me in his shaving mirror and turned 'round with a smile. I tried to ask if the rooms would be free for cleaning later on. He ignored me and said, "Constance has been in Scituate three days, tending the sick bed of her friend, Anne." I tried to leave then, but he was too fast for me. He grasped my arm. I wrenched myself away from him, but he would not accept my words of protest and flung me to the dressing-room sofa. He took me then, but I would not let him spend inside me—and instead pulled away at that moment, leaving him to stain my inside petticoats.

I spent the rest of the day in my rooms, trying not to think of my misfortunes. Alas, I failed.

June 20, 1868: He is the devil incarnate. Yet I cannot avoid him. As he cannot avoid me. Since that morning I came upon him shaving, he has followed me about the house. He came to me that night and again last night. He tells me that Constance is a young fool and he was a fool to marry her and not me but that he was deceived by her. Whenever he speaks, I know he is lying, but whenever he touches me, I feel as though the fevers of the scarlatina are upon me. He tells me we are bound to each other by bonds greater and more

lasting than any he has known—immortal ties. And I—fool that I am—I believe him.

God help me. Deliver me from this Satan!

Amity's torments and the affair continued for another month, detailed with increasing self-recrimination, unabated passion, and much accompanying calls for heaven's help. Suddenly, another type of entry—one long missing from Amity's diary—makes an eerie appearance:

August 23, 1868: Driven by the intense heat from my rooms to the garden for some refreshment, I was distracted by Saturn, who came to show me a problem with the phaeton he is to drive. It appears the rear wheel on the passenger's side has been loosened by overuse. The bolt—a twisted mess of forged iron—appears even to my uneducated eye to be frayed in the extreme. I sent him to the general store in Scituate for a new one, but as it is no longer manufactured, we must order directly from the manufacturer in Springfield, Massachusetts. I warned Saturn to lock up the phaeton and to use only the dogcart until this bolt is repaired.

August 26, 1868: Constance's friend Anne was taken quite suddenly today. A boy ran over with a message and has been resting in the spare bedroom from his exertions. He will stay with my Uncle Todd in Nansquett overnight. After dinner, Eugene will drive Constance to Scituate. When Saturn told him the dogcart is the only vehicle fit to be driven, Eugene raged at him and struck the poor old black with his riding crop on the shoulders. Eugene said he would have the phaeton or Saturn's hide. I signaled to the Negro to not protest. God forgive me, but I think that the bolt may give on the road and throw Constance out.

August 27, 1868: Once more God has seen fit to punish me.

As I hoped, the bolt on the phaeton did break off the rear wheel tonight as Eugene drove Constance to Scituate. But a perverse destiny rules my life. For the first wheel's bolt also snapped under the sudden pressure. The entire coach tipped into a ditch. Not only my sister, but also my beloved, my Eugene... I cannot write the words, but I must, for I am the cause of it... My Eugene too is now dead. So am I cursed. So will I remain cursed.

And there Amity's diaries ceased.

Or so I thought at first. For she had filled up some dozen volumes of the notebooks, and this entry arrived at almost the final blank page of the volume containing it. Once more, I ranged through her diaries, looking for later entries. All I found were earlier. Could she have ceased to write in her diary after that final catastrophe? It was possible. Yet, she had driven herself to faithfully record all that had happened to her up to that date. Why would she end there? Could an occupation of so many years—since she was a girl of sixteen—suddenly have ended? Somehow I couldn't believe it.

I suppose what I really wanted to know, now that I knew what had happened to her from her point of view, was what Amity thought, how she felt, after the deaths of her sister and Captain Calder. For me, fascinating as the other entries had been, none of them really explained to me how she went on living afterward. Had she adjusted to her life, and their deaths? Had she consciously become a recluse? Or had the small-minded society of the town forced her into that role? And most of all, I wanted to know why, after so many years of living, she finally threw herself into the well.

Living in her house, walking through the same rooms she had walked through, sitting at the same furniture she had sat at, made me feel that I could come closer to understanding Amity now that I had read her diaries. If only more volumes would appear. For I felt—no, I believed for certain—there were more volumes to her diary and that they held the key to her story and its

sad conclusion. What I'd already read was what I'd already heard of her life, years ago, on the shore-side
porch of Grandpa Lynch's house. Now I wanted to hear
the rest of her story—what I believed would be the real
story of Amity Pritchard.

I went through every volume of the various sets in
the library, looking for more volumes of the diary, hoping that somehow or other, another one or two would
show up, misplaced, misbound, somewhere. I found
nothing. Then I thought of all the various cases still un-
opened in the large basement under the house and
began to search those. I spent entire afternoons going
through the furniture drawers, pulling apart the lids of
steamer trunks and portmanteaus, half ripping the
shredded upholstery off couches and chairs, always expecting to find the missing volumes.

Naturally I was upset about this and found myself
thinking about it with unusual vehemence at all hours
of the day. Karen wasn't much help in cheering me up
either. For the first time since we had been together,
she could not share my intense interest in something.
But of course she had not read the diaries, although I
left the last vivid volume open for her. And she had not
heard Amity's story early on as I had: Why should I expect her to be as consumed with it as I was? Yet I did,
and I felt that she was not only not interested in Amity,
but less than interested in me too, for the first time

since we'd married. I accused her to myself of being aloof, distant.

Naturally her working was responsible for much of this. Since the Nansquett library had reopened, people had begun using it in droves. She'd even had to hire an assistant, Kitty Packer, the spinster sister of Etty, the owner of the dinette off Twill Road, the town's only claim to a restaurant. Even so, Karen found her work there tiring. And something else was preying on her mind, although she denied it, and just laughed at me when I tried to tease it out of her. But I could see it in her behavior—her sudden absentmindedness, her musings, her inattentiveness; some mornings I would come upon her standing stock-still looking up at the foyer skylight as though lost in another time.

Yet it was Karen who, without trying, came to provide me with the lost volumes of Amity's diaries and what was to be the beginning of our own sad drama.

13

It was on a Wednesday afternoon some three months after Chas's visit and my discovery of Amity's intensely revelatory diaries. I had been in and out of the first floor north wing dining room all that day, confirming specifications and plans with a carpenter and a plasterer who were restoring the magnificent oval-shaped room's beveled moldings. I had finally gotten somewhat settled back into the library when the phone began to ring downstairs. I waited a second after it had stopped, then it rang on my desk.

"Sit down, Roger! Something wonderful has just happened."

"Karen?" I asked. "What? What is it?"

"Just answer me three questions. I want to be perfectly sure," she said.

"All right. Shoot."

"The volumes of Amity's diaries—they're red morocco with a crosshatch pattern and dove gray vellum paper, yes?"

"You've found more?"

"Wait a minute. I haven't finished asking my questions. Do they have a circle watermark with a line across its diameter on the left-hand side of the page?"

"Wait a second. I'll check." I picked up one volume and held a page to the light. I'd never noticed the watermark before. Sure enough, it was a small circle with a line through it. "You *have* found more volumes!" I exclaimed.

"I want to be sure, though," she said, "so that you aren't disappointed. I know how much you wanted to find one. It's a single volume only. For the year 1873. Does that sound right?"

I did some quick calculations. "I guess. Although it isn't sequential. She was still alive then."

"And does she dot her *i*'s over the following letter?"

"Yes." My excitement was growing. "You have found it. It's Amity's!"

"Oh, Roger, I'm so glad."

"Where though, where did you find it?"

"It came from a whole truckload of old books that were in the stacks upstairs here in the library. They were her books. The ones the library originally opened with, even though she had set up the foundation several years before. Well, a lot of it was odd stuff—Victorian novelists you've never heard of and a great many very boring-looking sermons by divines once famous. But this one volume looked so much like those you keep on your desk all the time, I thought it might be hers... And it is. I'll bring it home with me tonight. There! It's in my cloth bag right now. You know I'll never forget that anywhere."

Karen and I talked another minute or two about other matters, then we hung up. I heard the carpenter call out something below, but he could wait a minute. Another volume of Amity's diaries! Not in sequence. There were four years still missing. Still it proved that she had gone on to keep diaries, which was what I had assumed. And if this one had turned up, others might turn up too. They might be lying on someone's bookshelf somewhere in the town without anyone's knowing about it. They might have been sold as part of a collection and sent to another city. I would have to advertise for them—first in Nansquett, then in the state. Eighteen seventy-three: That was two years before she died. The diary had to be useful in explaining those gaps in her life. Possibly even holding a clue to her death. Perhaps—but did I dare think it?—perhaps in this volume too I would discover a distillation of those years of hers since the deaths of Calder and Constance, in one solid, heady, concentrated draught.

I did finally remember to go downstairs to discuss

with the carpenter his ideas about replacing crown molding for that which had been destroyed over the years. But I felt so exulted by the prospect of another volume of Amity's diaries that I couldn't bring myself to go back up to the library and return to the monograph I was working on.

After an hour or so of restlessness, I decided I really couldn't wait until Karen came home. I'd have to go to get that last volume immediately—read it through as soon as possible. I felt like someone given the answers to a crossword puzzle they'd been torturing themselves over for months—I simply had to take a peek.

When I arrived at the Nansquett library, I didn't spot Karen right away, but Kitty Packer was at the checkout desk, trying to shush a string of pubescent girls, each with an armload of books, telling them to stay in line and that she'd get around to each of them. I went to the other side of the line and leaned over the desk.

"Mrs. Lynch in?" I asked. I didn't know Kitty, and I wasn't eager to start up an acquaintance under these conditions.

She looked up, irate and flustered at this new call on her limited attention. "Gone for the afternoon," she said, stamping a book card with great determination, making the bun at the back of her head wobble with her effort.

"Gone?" I asked to make certain.

"Gone," she confirmed. "Next one. Turn all the books the same way, Jean. It's more work for me otherwise."

"Did Mrs. Lynch happen to say where she was going?" I asked.

Kitty looked up at me for the first time. "Not a word, mister. If you're a friend, you'll find her with Mr. Lynch. They left together. As usual."

I couldn't make any sense out of that, unless Kitty thought I was a masher and was trying to bother Karen. Her last words were meant to warn me off.

"At what time did she leave?" I tried.

"Around three. If you'd care to leave your name, she'll be here around noon tomorrow when we open."

"No. Thank you, no."

I drove back to the house. I suppose I expected to see Karen's MG parked in the driveway, her just getting out of it, waving the volume of Amity's diary at me.

The car wasn't there. Only the half-ton pickup the workers had driven there. Had Karen gone shopping?

Of course Kitty might have been mistaken about Karen's leaving with a man. Or she might have left with an acquaintance, and Kitty had assumed it was me. But the way she had said "as usual" really threw me off: I'd never gone to pick Karen up at the library. Was I correct in thinking Kitty said that to dissuade me from following Karen? Or was it true that Karen did leave the library every day at three? If so, where did she go? She never got home until after six.

Steeped in questions, I walked in the front door of the house. With plasterers and carpenters coming and going all day, the door was always left open for them.

As I got into the foyer, I could hear some of the men talking and laughing loudly from the dining room. I was about to go in and ask them if Karen had stopped by only to drive off to find me again, when there was a sudden silence. Then I heard one of the men's voices raised indignantly, saying, "Well, he's going to find out sometime. Everyone else in town has known about it for the past three months."

"Who's going to tell him?" the plasterer, Rob, asked. "You, maybe?"

"No. Maybe a letter. You know one that you don't sign or something like that."

I froze with their words, then decided I had to know who they were talking about. I tiptoed back to the front door, slammed it shut, and strode directly into the dining room.

"How's it going?" I asked clumsily, focusing on Rob.

"All right," he said. Both men hastily turned back to their work, their expressions sour and their faces half-flushed.

"Any messages or phone calls while I was out?"

"No, nothing," Rob said, still uncomfortable.

I knew now it was me they were talking about.

"I won't be back for an hour or so," I said too quickly. "If you're done by then, just leave the door un-
locked."

They said they would, obviously relieved it was such
a short encounter with me.

I lingered in the room for another minute or two,
watching them impassively. I was trying to think what I
should do next, but I knew all too well.

Once back in the car, I didn't hesitate. I drove directly to the address the local phone directory listed for
Chas Lynch. I recalled Bud Bianchi earlier saying that
Chas had divided his house into a two-family dwelling.
The phone book didn't say which of the two floors he
lived on, and I wasn't certain I really wanted to know
either, but I was so afraid of the vague fears that were
filling my mind since I'd heard the two men talking in
the dining room that I held on to this one idea: Go to
Chas's house, see, just see, confirm for yourself.

An outside wooden stairway had been recently built
up to a little deck on one side of the house. Luckily, it
ran past a wall below with sliding glass doors. Inside
on the first floor I could see children's toys and clothing. The other family must live below, although no one
seemed to be home.

I ascended the stairs quickly. Only once there did I
wonder what to do next. The door was open, and a
locked louvered-glass door showed a portion of the up-

stairs apartment. I saw a neat, small kitchen with breakfast nook and an unexceptional corridor leading off
both left and right. I couldn't see any farther in either
direction. I moved aside to lean over the deck railing
on the right and made out through a high window a
modern Danish furniture set, the living room, and beyond it an archway, leading to other rooms. No way to
see into them from the deck, and no need to. No one
was at home. Kitty had made a mistake.

Then I saw Karen's bag. It was hung on the peg of a
clothes rack in the hallway between the living room
and the arch that led to what probably was a bedroom.
Next to it hung a cracked old leather jacket that Chas
had been wearing the day he came to see me at the
Pritchard place. I could see the volume of Amity's diary
sticking out over the lip of the already overstuffed bag.
My heart dropped like a lead weight to my feet, and I
almost lost my balance and fell off the deck.

It was more damning than if I'd seen them in bed
together. The casual way Karen's bag was hung there,
right next to Chas's jacket, as though she did it often—
"as usual," Kitty's words came back to me with an
awful and compelling force. For how long, in that inti-
mate relationship to Chas's jacket? Three months, the
plasterer had said without knowing I was listening.
Three months. Long enough to be casual.

Afraid that I would be caught by one of them suddenly coming out of the bedroom, I turned and leaped down the stairs, jumped into my car, and drove off.

It was only as I was turning into the driveway to my house that Chas's last words to me in the turret library came back and made sense. "Suit yourself," he had said. And I had read malice in those words without knowing how he would get back at me. But now I understood. I had spurned Chas, and like the child he still was, he had struck back at me through my most vulnerable spot—through Karen.

But she couldn't possibly care for Chas, I told myself. She might be enthralled by him, infatuated by him even, as I had once been so many years ago. But she would be intelligent enough to see Chas as he really was. All I had to do was not do anything stupid or sudden or violent. Of course, I would somehow or another let her know I knew about the affair, then count on her to end it and return to me. I couldn't believe she wouldn't return to me.

14

Once I'd made that decision, I felt calm. I remained calm and even cheerful when Karen came home that evening. I even managed not to flinch when she produced the volume of Amity's diaries from her bag with a great flourish. She'd run upstairs as she'd run into the house from her car, and she was still panting with the effort. All I could think of was how unlike an adulterous wife she looked at that moment: more like a schoolgirl with an excellent report card she wished to share. I kissed Karen, kissed the volume of the diaries, then kissed her again.

I suppose Karen expected me to open it and read it right then. But I put it next to its dozen precursor volumes on the shelf next to the big oak table and said it could wait. Meanwhile, we ought to celebrate her finding it. First with a drink in the breakfast room downstairs, then I had an even better idea. There was a new roadhouse in the area with a reputation for excellent Continental cuisine. It would be only an hour's drive to Point Judith. We'd dine there tonight.

Karen was surprised, also pleased. I tried to treat the book as an excuse for the celebration, rather than as its cause. It wasn't merely that I hoped to create guilt in Karen, but I did want her to appreciate me more. I don't know if that was the result that night, but Karen was in one of her brightest moods, and dinner was perfect. Afterward we strolled along the shore. A full moon was rising—almost red it was so orange—out of the south, over the ocean. I felt no qualms about using its romantic effect, taking Karen in my arms and kissing her. She responded instantly, totally, almost with relief, I thought, and we made love right there in the dunes, surrounded by driftwood and dried seaweed thrown up by an earlier tide, with Karen's dress pushed up and my pants down at my feet, like the forbidden teenage lovers we never were. Both of us were terribly excited, and she was so loud in her pleasure when she began to orgasm that I thought for certain we would draw the attention of some of the night surf fishers we'd seen walking.

If I was to win Karen back, I had to show her not only that I cared for her more than Chas but that I could provide as much interest in her life. I thought that one reason she'd begun seeing him was to counteract the tedium that had set into her life once we'd moved to Nansquett and begun restoring the house. I blamed myself for paying too much attention to restoring the Pritchard house and not enough to making my marriage with Karen a happy, growing one.

Thereafter, acting swiftly and without warning, I spent the next few weeks keeping her interested, amused, busy. I would arrive at the library at 2:30 in the afternoon and ask Karen to come with me to an auction of old furniture I'd read about in Newport. I knew she loved auctions and old furniture. I would have the opportunity of scouting through any book lots for possible missing diary volumes, and Karen could always bid on one or two things, like the lovely bowed-front music-sheet cabinet she picked up, now sitting in the music room next to a huge Boston fern.

Or we would suddenly go to Mystic for the afternoon and wander around the Connecticut seaport, restored to its nineteenth-century state. I took her to the Rocky Point amusement park I recalled my parents taking me to as a boy, and I thrilled her with a ride on the rickety old roller coaster. One afternoon I asked Karen if I could check through the reserves of the Nansquett public library on the off chance she had missed another volume of Amity's diaries. She couldn't say no, and she had to remain at the front desk, lest I suddenly came upstairs and found her gone. Another day I insisted that she stay at home when the architect came to discuss our plans for restoring the last few rooms of the house—the bedrooms on the north side of the house. In those weeks we drove over most of the state of Rhode Island and into neighboring states. But we didn't go out every afternoon, not only because that would be too obviously a demand on her time but because I wanted Karen to have time with Chas so that she could compare our relationships. However, we did make love on almost all of these excursions—and always under what I considered to be unusual circumstances: in the back of my car parked under a train trestle one night; in a motel in a small town in Massachusetts, where the owner eyed us suspiciously even when we showed him credit cards with matching names.

Karen never questioned, hesitated, or failed to agree to one of these suddenly inspirational adventures with me. She would enter into each of them with almost adolescent delight. I had to remind myself on more than one occasion that her girlish delight was indeed girlish—after all she was only twenty-two years old, I almost thirty. I could almost picture her face as she told Chas one day, "What am I supposed to do? Say no? After all, he is my husband." I remembered how much of a physical narcotic my own time with Chas had been, and I tried to wean her off that by narcotizing her to me instead. The more I experimented with new sexual techniques with Karen, the more she responded and the more interested I became. I even took her to a pornographic movie house in downtown Providence one afternoon, making love to her with my fingers while we sat side by side in the smoky, silent, sleazy theater darkness, broken only by the flickering of the screen and an infrequent and almost inadvertent moan from one of the shadowy figures placed distant from us and each other. And it worked, all of it. We were closer than we'd ever been. True, every once in a while I would catch Karen staring at me obliquely in store window reflections as we window-shopped, in hallway full-length mirrors as we prepared to go out. But she'd always looked at me that way, in sidelong glances. And being with her so much more made her even more precious to me, if only because of her willingness to allow herself to be won back.

I capped the assault on her with a vacation at Provincetown, where we'd passed our belated honeymoon. If it was only one week long instead of the month of the previous year, it was because I wanted to return to the restoration of the house and to the turret library to check up on some of Amity's references, not because Karen was rushing back to her paramour.

Coming home, we took the same road we'd taken from the Cape the year before. As we pulled off the highway and onto Atwood Avenue, I slowed down and pulled up opposite our driveway.

"The FOR SALE sign was right there," I said, pointing. "Do you remember?"

Karen remembered and kissed my neck under my ear. I was certain I'd succeeded in winning her back.

15

We had taken my car on the trip to the Cape because Karen had complained of the brakes seeming loose on her MG.

The day after our return to Nansquett, I walked to the library, picked up her car, and drove it to the Scituate auto-repair garage where Chas worked. I had called him up earlier that day to ask if he would look at the MG's brakes, and he was so surprised to hear from me, he'd done the unforgivable for an auto mechanic: He said he would check them that day.

Chas wasn't in the garage when I drove in. Another older man named Jake—Chas's business partner—put the car on the hoist and lifted it almost to the ceiling, telling me that my cousin was at lunch nearby.

I had calculated on being in Scituate for a few hours at least while the brake inspection was going on and had gotten together a list of miscellaneous shopping I'd been putting off for months. When I got most of that done and arrived back at the garage, it was after five. Jake was gone and would be back to take over the evening shift: The trousered legs that stuck out from under the MG turned out to belong to Chas. He'd been lying on his back on a flat dolly and slid out from under the car when he heard me come in. His shirt was off, his torso covered with blond hair and motor oil. He looked up at me, half squinting, as though blinded by the light after the dimness of a small lightbulb under the car's chassis.

"Hi!" he said. I wasn't certain he recognized me.

"What's the verdict?" I asked, nodding at the car.

"I'll have to get a part for it. I don't have it. I'll have to order it from a foreign car dealer in Providence. Jake is going up there tonight. He'll pick it up. I'll be ready tomorrow afternoon. Sorry for the delay."

"Great!" I said. I had been too optimistic. I had three shopping bags full of my day's purchasing in Scituate. "Is there a cab service I can call to get all this home?"

Chas frowned and stood up. "If you can wait fifteen minutes until Jake gets back, I'll drive you home. I'm off then."

"I'll wait," I said. I wanted to spend some time with him, to gauge his reactions, to hear what, if anything, he had to say—possibly to hear him foolishly incriminate himself.

He didn't. He was silent during our drive to Nansquett. I decided that I would bring it all to a head on
my own. Not alone, but with Karen. We were having a
roast for dinner. There was certainly enough for three.
I invited him to dine with us, insisted he dine with us,
told him Karen had asked me more than once why my
only cousin in the place had never come by for a social
evening. I knew he hadn't seen her in more than a
week—all the time we'd been away—and would jump at
the chance. But he was clever. He claimed he had
studying to be done, and I had to persuade him out of
his reluctance. By the time we'd arrived at the Twill
Road exit off the highway, he'd accepted, making it
seem a favor to me, and said he'd drop me off and then
go home to clean up.

   I thought that was an excuse to not show up for dinner and told him it was foolish to drive me to my
house, then double back and then come back. We were
right near where he lived. We could stop off there, and
I'd wait until he was ready. Then, too, I believed in that
moment that I was the winner, he the loser; and win-
ners can afford to be generous to losers.

   Winner or not, I wasn't prepared for the sudden lack
of assurance I experienced ascending those stairs outside his house, unable to forget my first ascent and
what I had discovered at the top of the stairs.

   Chas left me in the living room with some year-old

copies of *Playboy* and stacks of modern issues of electronics magazines to browse through while he bathed.

I couldn't remain seated, however, and began to walk around the apartment to dispel my restlessness. I idly inspected every piece of furniture, every one of the few decorations he had, torturing myself with wondering whether it had already been there three and a half months ago or whether Karen had seen it and bought it for the apartment. It was a crazy thing to do but something I couldn't help. She'd been in these rooms. She'd sat on this chair, probably at this table, having a cup of coffee before coming home to me. She left her bag on that hook next to where he'd tossed his leather jacket when he'd come in with me. She'd probably looked in that small oval mirror, brushing her hair. Under this arch she'd more than likely undressed. She'd lain on that bed, invitingly. How invitingly. Or she'd sat on this low upholstered chair in his bedroom. I sat in it too, looking around, conjuring her presence at the bureau or on the bed—doing what? What had she and Chas done that she and I never did?

I was startled into the present by Chas himself, stepping out of the bathroom that adjoined the bedroom. He was naked and clean, toweling his long wet hair. He stopped at the doorway but kept rubbing his hair dry. Then he smiled at me with that same lopsided grin filled with meaning that I hadn't seen in years. With his

clothing off, Chas looked slighter, fragile, more vulnerable than in the turret library—almost a boy again.

"Comfortable?" he asked with all kinds of innuendo.

"Very," I answered. My voice had taken on that same tone of secrecy. Thinking of Karen and Chas together in that room had excited me. Looking at Chas's body now, in the orange glow of the setting sun, I felt a perverse attraction for him.

"C'mere," I said.

His smile widened. "I thought you didn't do that anymore," he said. "It's unnatural, remember?"

That slight resistance made me want to see him down on me, giving me back what he'd taken from me through Karen.

"C'mere," I said, holding out my arms to him.

He came slowly, warily to where I sat, and I took his forearms, lightly caressing them, then suddenly pulling them toward me, until he stumbled and fell onto one knee in front of me. I reached over and pressed down on his shoulders, bringing him to both knees.

"Maybe my memory is too short," I said in a low voice. "Why don't you remind me of what I'm missing."

I unzipped and, grabbing his curly drying hair, pressed him down into my lap. He resisted at first, and I jerked his head back and slapped his face once—hard. It was more than enough. His eyes smoked up at me as he pulled my pants down over my knees, and I caressed

his golden curls until I began to feel the burning wetness of ejaculation welling up in me. It was intense,
perhaps the most intense orgasm of my adulthood.

"You were always the best, Chas," I told him when he
had pulled away and leaned against the side of the bed.
His stomach was streaked from his own discharge, and
he stared at the floor without speaking.

Now I'm satisfied, I thought, standing up, pulling up
my pants, and buckling myself. *Now we're even.* But I
didn't say it aloud; I still wanted to be able to lean over
the dinner table in front of Karen and show her in
some way.

Chas dressed as though for visiting and drove me
home. He even helped me take the various bags out of
the car. But when I turned around to suggest he park
right where he was, he turned his car around in the dirt
road and sped off, sending fans of dirt high into the air.

16

I had begun to read through the newly found volume of Amity's diary the day after Karen brought it home. The earlier dozen or so tomes were filled with domestic incidents, home remedies, and then the swiftly moving, precisely accounted story of the Pritchard sisters and Captain Calder's triangle with its tragic aftermath, which had made for easy, fast reading. Not this volume. By the time we'd returned to Nansquett from Cape Cod, I'd managed to get through about two thirds of the volume. After that late afternoon with Chas, I finally felt settled down enough about him and Karen and me to involve myself in Amity's diary once more and read it right to the end.

I had expected to find a different person in her writing than the tormented, passion-driven, and destiny-buffeted Victorian heroine of the earlier volumes I had read and reread so many times, I could probably repeat some entries verbatim. But whatever I had prepared myself for, I was in for a shock.

In the five years since the deaths of Constance and Eugene Calder, Amity Pritchard had become a recluse, never venturing into Nansquett, often sending Saturn, her Negro servant, and finally having deliveries sent to the entranceway of the property from the dry-goods and general stores of the town. That much I already knew from Grandfather's telling, years before. What I hadn't known—and really couldn't have known—was that other deliveries were made to the Pritchard property too: not from Nansquett or even from Scituate but from several of the largest bookstores in the East, in New York, in Providence, and mostly from the flourishing Brattle Book Store in Boston, gathering place of Back Bay bluestockings and the Concord Transcendentalists, Orientalists, and Theosophists.

True to her upbringing and earliest inclinations, once she was thrown on her own again Amity began to delve into philosophy. Like her father—the Reverend Pritchard—she came to all but live in the turret library, where, day by day, again like her father, she sought answers to the curious fate that had befallen her. Unlike the Reverend, however, Amity did not peruse the scriptures and Apocrypha or glosses on these works by learned men of earlier ages. She delved into the esoteric—the Bhagavadgita, the teachings of Lao Tsu and

Chuang Tse, and the Hindu texts of the Upanishads—
all newly translated and much talked about in the finest
intellectual circles of Cambridge, Concord, and New
York in her time. How she had come to know of these
works, she never wrote. But by the time she came to
write her last diary, she had read and reread these
works, digested them, cogitated upon them, and was
ready to synthesize their wisdom into a meaningful pattern that would explain, if not propitiate.

She devoted pages and pages of densely packed
meditations to an acceptance of a theory of time and
space, and the place of human life in that nexus, which
was partly the result of her reading and partly what
amounted to an almost Einsteinian speculation of the
nature of the universe.

"Time is like the coils of a spring," she wrote in one
entry. "When the spring is stretched out, each coil is a
graceful individual arc with an elegance of form determined by its beginning out of a previous accumulation
of other arcs, reaching toward an apex or climax and
gracefully curving back to end in a future accumulation
of arcs. Each life is such an arc—separate yet connected.
Each consciousness is such an arc too, only one of
many undergone in varying shapes and circumstance
and in several places by the same soul."

A striking image, to show her belief in reincarna-
tion—an unusual enough belief for a New England

spinster daughter of a preacher yet not all that rare in her time. Yet, listen how later on in this entry she leaped ahead of all of her peers:

Our perceptions show that while years and days and hours are as rigidly marked off as the metal of a spring's coil, yet that they vary, due to ourselves and our circumstances. Time is passed in happiness races ahead, waits, then snaps back in an instant. Seconds can become years, but some years—especially passed in despair—can become as centuries.

Surely she had been ahead of Bergson with this understanding. But there was still a fuller synthesis to be made.

Being fluid like water, only finer by far, yet rigid like a metal coil, there are areas where the coil snaps back from being stretched to twisting—as it must recoil before being stretched again. Ideally, these are noted by the points of birth and death, when the soul clearly begins or completes an arc and the coil must be stretched again for the soul to relive. Yet there are other points within each arc— less noticeable than such monuments as birth and death, when the arc wavers, the stretching gives way, and in a trice the coil snaps suddenly shut. All sensitive people have noticed these times—we call them supernatural to explain them. Though they are natural enough, simply extraordinary by their manner of defying the natural tension of the arc of life. When we dream a dream that later comes true or guess a guess that is later proved so or feel familiar with a place where we have never been before and could not know, it is because of this minor relaxation of the coil back to its place of rest.

An exploration of ESP years before it was even recognized? I read on and discovered the clincher.

Material is carried from life to life, from arc to arc of the coil. The most energetic material always reoccurs. This the Hindus called Karma. It happens in our time and space as the most sudden and unsuspecting snapping of the coil before it turns and tenses again. That is how one life can affect the next—how the past can become a new present. If this energy is malevolent or irksome, we suffer; if benevolent, we take joy. As all lives are such coils intertwined and interconnected at arcs, when, for example, two or three or more of the coils snap to a rest at one time, a previous situation involving all of them can become a present situation.

That year and a half between Captain Calder,

Constance, and me contained all the prerequisites
of such a situation—great passion, inexplicable
sudden attractions, inability to obtain full and lasting satisfaction through more conventional chan-
nels, isolation from the rest of society. It was, in
short, what the Hindus would call a 'karmic' situation—a sudden snapping of the arcs of all three of
our interrelated coils.

So Amity had synthesized it—or at least come to
terms with it. And in so doing, she came to also predict:

If this has occurred in the middle of this, the nineteenth century after the death of our Lord, it means
that such a situation has happened before; how
else explain how we three could be so prepared for
it, so ready to act it out, despite our ordinarily dif-
fering personalities, our wishes, our ideas, our cus-
toms and traditions? And if it has happened twice,
it will happen once more—at least—some time in
the future, long after I too am dead and forgotten.
For no solution was achieved this time; no, only
more crime and sorrow and foolishness perpetuat-
ed. So I believe it *must* happen again to once more
have the opportunity for solution. Whether in
twenty years or fifty or five hundred I cannot know.
I have done what I could. I will go on doing what

I can to understand all this, to ready myself and my soul for that next recurrence. For it is like a twist in the coils, a blot on the universal harmony, and it has to be eliminated once and for all, the twisted path made straight, the arcs smoothed, the lives made peaceful and prosperous.

That, then—after untold, undigested rehashings of earlier teachings—was how Amity had adjusted or, rather, how she had come to rationalize what had happened in her life. Yet hopeful as her writings were, they still failed to explain her suicide. Before I could reach that point, I had to read entry after entry in her increasingly crabbed handscript to make certain I understood what she had concluded. For with this volume of the diary, I began to have a faint conception that her life and the conclusions she reached about it were not only important to her but also crucial to me. As yet I could not—I did not want to—consolidate my thoughts on this. But when I came to her December 9 entry, I had to stop, short of breath, from reading it over and over.

December 9, 1873: I left the house for the first time in five years today. It was for the christening of my cousin Anthony Todd's firstborn son. Ordinarily, I would not attend such an occasion, but all this past week I have felt something important for

my life—not this one but the one to come after I have shed this body—will result should I decide to go to the church. Accordingly, I dressed in my best remaining clothes—although a funeral black—and had Saturn drive me.

Once there, it seemed I had been mistaken. Only the Todd and Rance families from New Bedford attended, and they all were clustered around the baptismal font. I remained as far back from them as possible, alert in all of my senses for what I felt might occur of importance to me.

Finally it did, although like all of life, in a manner at first odd to me. A boy about eight years old, dressed neatly in a serge suit, had been looking at me for so long that I looked back at him. He wasn't merely curious or suspicious of me either, as I at first thought. When I glanced at him a second time, he smiled at me. I haven't see such an innocent smile in years, and it refreshed my soul to see him. I motioned him over and leaned my hand on his strong young shoulder to support myself during the preacher's interminable sermon, allowing the boy to steal what I can with no vanity call admiring gazes at me. When the service had been performed, I gave the boy a small gift to bring up to the font. I felt it was he—this boy—I had come to see, to somehow impress, not my relatives. Then I left the church.

Once settled in the phaeton, I had new doubts.
I was now certain the boy was the link I needed to
my new life, though how he was I could not say for
certain. Had I sufficiently impressed the boy, I
asked myself. For I felt that was necessary above
all. Then I spotted him on the vestry steps, looking
out the doorway. I called to him, asking his name,
thanked him for his service to me, and in a flash I
decided to make certain he would always remember me. I gave him a shiny five-dollar gold piece.

As I thought, the boy was flabbergasted. I said
one or two more words of little importance to him,
then tapped the carriage side for Saturn to drive
off. Returning home, I felt a new peace descend
upon me. I am now certain this boy—this young
Ralph Lynch—is my vital, my all important link to
a future life.

There Amity's diaries ended. Ended with a year or so
left for her to live; ended with her suicide still unexplained; ended with too many blank leaves remaining
in the notebook for me to be certain that she really intended that last entry to be her last words, her last writing, her epitaph somehow. Ended with her meeting my
Grandpa Lynch as a little boy, a meeting he had remembered very well, never forgotten, which he had
told me about and caused me to come to see Amity's

house for the first time, to live here again years later, and to bring Karen here so she might begin an affair with my cousin Chas Lynch. It ended so I could know after reading it that Amity had been correct, that her situation would come up again, a little more than a hundred years later, in Nansquett once more. And that Karen and Chas and I would replace and replay the roles of Constance and Eugene Calder and Amity, come back somehow in the great dice throw of existence to work out this awful connection all three of us had one more time—for good this time: to get that twist out of the coil, to reestablish a harmonious universe. And to do it all with one extraordinary advantage that none of them had had in their time—we had Amity's story to read, Amity's understanding of it to guide us, to keep us from falling into the same ghastly, wasteful, foolish mistakes they—and especially she—had made.

17

"Don't you see, Karen? If you do what you're planning to, you'll only be repeating it—betraying all those years of Amity's suffering, ignoring the wisdom she finally accumulated out of that suffering for us!"

It was raining so hard outside the breakfast room, I almost had to shout to be heard over the downpour. Great sheets of rain fell in swirling gusts, splashing first against one window, then turning back to smash across another one. We were having a late-morning lunch—a silent, tense, desolate meal, until I decided to talk.

Karen's raincoat was thrown across one chair, still dripping wet from our one quick walk down to her car an hour before. I'd helped her put the two suitcases she had packed that morning into the trunk of her MG, returned, repaired, from Chas's Scituate garage yesterday afternoon. Nothing had been really said between us. She'd spent the night out, only coming back to the

house at nine o'clock—awakening me in the turret library, where I had fallen asleep over some of Amity's
diaries. I was barely able to understand Karen's words
when she shook me gently and said she had to go to
New York that day.

Then I understood all too well. Somehow the day
before, Chas had demanded she make a choice. He'd
persuaded her to come to him yesterday afternoon,
persuaded her to stay over for the night, and persuaded her to drive away with him today: to leave me. And
there she was, a little frightened but also very determined, standing hesitantly in the library, telling me she
was leaving me without meaning any harm in it, as
though she were telling me she was going to see a den-
tist or going to see a show.

I'd wanted to say something then: something angry
and bitter and very cruel. I wanted to expose Chas, to
show her the kind of man he was—if he could even be
called a man. But I held back. I went down to the
kitchen and brewed some coffee and, sipping from my
cup, watched the rain begin to fall. Then I went upstairs again with a cup for her. I watched her throw
clothing out of drawers and closets onto the bed and
then fill up the two suitcases she'd received as a wedding present from an aunt in New York, and I never
said a word.

Wordless still, I helped Karen bring them downstairs

and put them into the MG. Then I walked a step or two behind her back up into the house and into the breakfast room, where we sat down and looked out at the rain falling heavier every moment, it seemed, whipping branches of trees almost to the ground.

It was then that I broke the silence. I knew that to argue with her, to say anything directly touching the situation, would only harden her in her determination to go with Chas. I was shocked by her decision. Its suddenness after these weeks of relative calm—especially after I felt I had won her back—unnerved and disturbed me. She couldn't have made the decision earlier—she'd seen so little of Chas in the past month, spent so much time with me instead. I suppose that was what had spurred him on, that and our encounter in his bedroom, which I had intended to humiliate and yet satisfy him: I'd succeeded only in humiliating him, in determining him on his vengeful course. Disappointed as I was, I refused to fall prey to his game—I would do anything before I would jump feet first into the role he had prepared for me: that of irate abandoned husband.

That's why I talked about Amity, telling Karen what I knew of her and Captain Eugene Calder and Constance, repeating their story as Grandpa Lynch had told it to me, then as I had discovered it myself through Amity's journals. I repeated almost verbatim the conclusions Amity had reached, her understanding of the situation, her prophecy of the future in that last volume, the one Karen herself had found for me. I talked as calmly and quietly as the noise of the inclement weather outside would allow, feeling as though I were telling a fairy tale to a sleepy, recalcitrant child but stressing it too, for she had to understand what was happening to her, so that by being aware of all of it, she could come to a more mature decision.

We sat there more than an hour. We'd finished eating long before. We lingered. Karen, I know, was waiting for Chas to arrive; I was trying to change our circumstances through her in that remaining time.

"So you see, Karen, *we* are Constance and Amity and Calder: you and I and Chas. The situation is too close to be merely coincidental, too filled with correspondences to be only an accident. Can you believe that, Karen?"

She looked at me for a second with an indefinable gaze, then turned away to the window, showing me her profile. Two strands of hair had fallen across her forehead, and she didn't even lift them up into place. She was thinking, thinking hard; either that or not thinking at all—merely staring at me through the reflection of the glass.

"Well?" I insisted. "Do you believe me?"

"I don't know, Roger," she said, not to me directly but to my reflection, to the rain outside. "I don't really understand what those people dead a hundred years have to do with us."

"They have everything to do with us! It's a pattern that repeats: like the pattern of waves in the ocean. Unless the pattern is broken, it'll just go on and on forever. Can't you see that?"

"Patterns. Can't you think of anything else?" she said, sounding weary suddenly and unsure of herself. She was reproaching me for the first time since we'd met, and I was stung by it—oddly stung, since so much worse was in store for both of us if I couldn't convince her to remain.

"No, that isn't all I can think of. It isn't all. You must know that."

Karen stood up and went to the tallest of the half-dozen windows, nervously tapping on a pane, impatient for Chas to come, impatient for it to be done.

"What will you do now?" I asked quietly, trying to change the subject for a minute from my real concern.

"Go back to the reference room, I guess."

"And Chas? What about him?"

"He said he has some friends who have an electronics repair business. They'll hire him."

"It will be difficult," I said tonelessly. "You won't have much money to live on, will you?"

"It will be difficult," she replied, toneless as I was. "But everything seems difficult anyway. Roger? Roger, don't hate me. Don't think of me as a tramp or... I couldn't bear to have you think that way about me. That I'm really only a tramp, that... Oh, never mind."

"Karen, darling," I said, getting up and going to where she stood, framed by the window, defined by the sheets of rain in the trees outside. "You don't really want to go," I said as gently as I knew how. I held her shoulders, breathing in her smell of fresh shampoo and rinse, and she didn't flinch from me. "Chas wants you to go. But you don't really want to. I know how he can be. I was once under his control. I was. When I was only a boy. I know how it is. I'll help you to regain yourself, Karen."

"You *can't* know."

"But I do. It was no different with me. Believe me."

She half turned, half faced me, then turned back to the window, watching for him.

"The terrible thing," she said, "the really awful thing is that I almost believe you when you talk like that— about us being Amity and her sister and that Captain. Not that I feel as though I was any of them—which of them would I have been, Roger? But this house, this town, it seemed so familiar, so already known to me, right from the beginning. Do you remember? It's been like living in a perpetual déjà vu with no real sense of time passing all the months we've been here, restoring the house. Why else would that be?"

"I don't know. Subconscious memory or something," I replied.

"Everyone talks about us, Roger," she went on, once more changing the subject. "I don't mind for my sake or for Chas's. But it makes me feel so bad for you when I know they're gossiping and slandering you."

"Then you do care for me. A little?"

"I wouldn't have married you otherwise," she said. "But it isn't the same as with Chas. It's almost as though you and I grew up together, as though you were my older brother, showing me things, teaching me." She sighed. I wanted to say something but held back for a minute, letting her go on. "Maybe it's because I never *can* feel time the right way here that I have to leave. Everything feels so vague here, so let loose from things that count, that ought to count. Maybe that's why I'm doing this. Because it's something definite in the middle of so much vagueness. I feel like I've been living in a dream with you, Roger. Right from the day you came over to me with that silly message on the call slip in the library. Like a very lovely dream, but a very strange dream too. Very strange, Roger."

"It's because of the past. Just as Amity wrote. Because we forged links in the past—before we even were, Karen."

"It's not a dream with Chas, though," she said, her voice becoming hard. "It's real with him. I feel as though I'm touching ground, touching something solid, even though it is squalid. He's real enough, Roger. He has faults. He's stupid, he's inconsiderate at times, selfish, so selfish and demanding and nasty sometimes. You're not like that, Roger. You're too good to be true. That's the awful thing. I can't believe you are real, Roger. I just can't. And I can't feel real with you."

"Karen, darling, I have faults too. I have eccentricities by the score."

"But you aren't callous or brutal or… And life is brutal, Roger. People are callous. That is real. This, well, this has been lovely, this house like a huge playhouse," she said, her voice beginning to quiver. "Roger, hold me, talk to me, talk to me about Amity and Calder again, persuade me, argue with me, hit me, lock me up, do something, anything. Please, darling, please!"

Her sudden outburst after so much restraint shocked me. But I held her, as she asked, held her close to me, whispering into her ear I don't know what nonsense, kissing her hair, holding on to her body as though for dear life, hoping, hoping. And all the while she cried softly, and the rain tore in sheets around the house.

All of a sudden she jerked upright in my arms as though stung. One minute, all of her relaxed and frail; the next minute, all rigid and tense.

Then I too heard the car horn honking. I tried to keep holding her, but she looked up now, and as close as she still was to me in my arms, she was no longer with me. I let her remove my arms from her waist and shoulder, let her push me aside and step to the other window, where she peered down through the rain. The car honked again, and she began to wave down, as though with exaggerated effort. I knew in that second that she was lost.

She'd already turned to the table, found a handkerchief in her purse, and dried her eyes. The compact clicked open. She dabbed herself lightly. It clinked shut. She put it back into the purse and put on the raincoat, draped over the back of one chair. She slung the purse over her shoulder and stood there, biting her lower lip.

"Good-bye, Roger. And thank you. It's been a lovely dream. I'll never forget it."

I followed her out of the room mechanically, down the stairs into the foyer, and took her arm. She didn't shake me off.

"Get a raincoat or umbrella or something if you're coming out," she said.

"I'm all right," I replied.

We walked arm and arm out the front door and over to the retaining wall. Chas was waiting in the front seat of his car, the windshield wipers flashing off thin sheets of rain with every moment, like a cat shaking itself. Karen preceded me down the stone steps. I took her arm again at the bottom, and we walked to his car.

Chas had gotten out and stood watching us approach—curious and even a little suspicious.

"Where are your bags?" he shouted over the rain. He couldn't hide the doubt in his voice.

"I thought we'd take my car," she said almost humbly—a tone of voice I'd never heard her use with me. "It's a long trip. Didn't you just overhaul it?"

"The bags are in the trunk," I said to him.

Chas looked at me for the first time, as though only just seeing me with Karen. I couldn't tell what he was thinking.

"Hello, Roger," he said, and when I didn't reply, he turned to the backseat of the car and began to take out the two suitcases he had. "Will you let this stay here until someone comes to pick it up?" he asked, meaning the car. I didn't answer but helped him with one of the bags, stuffing it behind the seat of the MG's single seat.

Karen reached up and touched my cheek. Rain was beginning to streak her hair. I opened the passenger side door, and she got in without a word.

"I've never seen a rainstorm like this," Chas was saying. "The roads are going to be flooded."

He got into the MG then, and I stood back against the doors of the old stable we'd transformed into a garage. Rain was slashing along the car windows, obscuring my last look at Karen. Chas was talking to her, and she seemed to be looking down at her lap, as though listening.

I half raised my hand to wave as he revved the car up, but a sheet of rainwater tore across the top of the garage and nearly knocked me against the garage doors. When I'd recovered, the MG was gone, tearing around the bend of the road leading to Atwood Avenue, sending up long flashes of water from the gullies.

I watched its path for some time, until I began to realize I was shivering: soaked through. Walking back up those steps to the Pritchard house was the longest walk I could remember. Back inside I stripped off my clothing, wrapped myself in a blanket, and lit a fire in the bedroom fireplace. Chill had already begun to set in. Even with a brandy, I felt cold. I got into the huge bed we'd shared and shook with cold until I fell asleep.

18

Javanese bells tinkled through my dreams—silvery and almost immaterially sweet but insistent too.

I started up, recognizing the front door chimes. From my bedroom window I couldn't see anyone outside, but they would be sheltered by the doorway overhang anyway. It seemed already dark, although my dresser clock read only three o'clock.

I dressed, listening to the chimes ring on, and rushed downstairs through the darkened house, throwing on light switches as I ran, vaguely hoping it was Karen returning to me.

Two state police stood huddled in the overhang of the doorway, their raincoats black and shiny with the wetness. The rain had stopped, but the woods were still crackling and dripping with its fall.

The two men almost didn't have to speak to tell me what I knew already the instant I opened the front door and saw them. The MG had swerved to avoid another car coming the wrong way off the highway exit, they told me. The brakes must not have held, the policemen supposed. The MG had hit an abutment, then veered over the cross lane directly into an oncoming truck. Chas and Karen had died instantly. I was needed to identify what remained of them.

EPILOGUE

After the men from Scituate had repaired the well, I put on a heavy jacket and went to inspect their work. A good job, very professional. They told me it would be a few days before the well filled up again, the water seeping upward from the springs in the ground. Perhaps a week, they said, wondering without saying it why anyone would want such an impractical, old-fashioned well repaired again. But by the time I went to look at it, less than an hour after they had gone, the water had begun to enter: I could see an inch or so of it covering the bottom layer of new bricking they had laid, creeping slowly upward—clear water, fresh spring water from the earth, from the rain we've had so much of this year. As though the well were a sensate thing and knew why I had to have it repaired, knew the part it would once again play in the eternal drama, even if they—the men from Scituate, the townspeople of Nansquett—do not know.

My only consolation is that I didn't do what I might have done out of anger and ignorance and frustration. I didn't fight Chas and Karen's being together—I simply tried to stop it, tried to stop them from going away. I didn't allow the carriage bolts to remain unrepaired. I had the MG brakes fixed, unconscious of what I was doing. It was Chas himself who somehow failed to ensure that those brakes would hold. Not I. And that consoles me, telling me that some of the twists in the coil that Amity wrote of have been made straight, telling me that while the situation was the same and even the way in which they died appallingly similar, that details have changed.

Because now, even without having Amity's own words, her own explanation for it, I have come to understand why she went to her well for surcease. In those quiet autumn days after Chas and Karen were buried in the Nansquett cemetery (as close to Amity and Constance and Eugene Calder as I could place them), I still sought reasons for her act, still questioned my own acts before their deaths to discover if I could have done something, if things could have been different.

Less than a year later, I know: I no longer ask questions. The change was not a dramatic one—this sudden understanding—but a seeping one, as though the very rooms of this house, the shape of the furniture, the books, the trees outside hold the answer and are imparting it to me every instant of my life. As though every creaking of the wooden frame over the turret in a wind, every sweep of a breeze through the branches or tiny crackle of a twig as I roam the woods around the house are offering me the answer—quietly, uninsistently, yet with a growing definition and assurance I cannot deny.

Of course I was alone by the time I made my discovery—quite alone. The house was restored—every detail in place—no more workmen to come and disturb me with their buzz saws and hammers, with their cursing and yells. Once Karen and Chas were buried and no one from town had any reason to call on me, I was blessedly able to concentrate on listening to what the house and its surroundings had to tell me. I was able to listen, to eventually hear and understand that what had happened before had happened now twice and that it would have to happen once more, whether twenty years or fifty years or five hundred years from now: three of us bound by spiritual love and sensual passion spinning toward consummation one more time. Subtly changed, as ours had been subtly changed from Amity's situation; the explosiveness of our coming together defused even more than we three had defused from its original mold. Perhaps when it occurred again it would be shot through with understanding, not from only one of us—as this time—but by all of us. After all,

we had acted it out almost as though we were mari-
onettes, without great force. Karen and I—at least—had
gone further: We had questioned it, stood back, and
tried to observe it. We failed, but at least we didn't add
another twist to the coil through violence and stupidi-
ty but perhaps straightened out the coil, if only by the
tiniest fraction.

The next time it happens—and I now have no doubt
that it will happen again—perhaps the twist will be so
small as to hardly have an effect. We will be even more
aloof from passion then, more understanding of each
other, more evolved—Constance and Eugene and I,
Karen and Chas and I—more ready to love as three,
without rancor, without separation.

I already feel the contact to that future has been
made. A week before the men from Scituate came to repair the well, I thought I had established the link. Now
I'm certain.

The little girl was waiting at the entrance to the dirt
road leading to the house. Just standing there, frightened but fascinated too, holding a square brown paper
parcel in her hands, trying to gather up the courage to
come in, standing there I don't know how long, perhaps only a few minutes, perhaps an hour.

She was startled when I stepped out of one of the
side paths and waved to her. Then she caught herself
and thrust the parcel forward, staring at me the way

adolescent girls stare at movie stars and rock stars—
with awe and fear and longing. She spoke quickly, quietly, yet breathing hard all the while, as though she had
not been standing still when I came upon her but running. Her aunt, she said, had sent her on the errand.
She had lovely blue-green eyes and straight auburn
hair, very pretty, about twelve or thirteen years old, I
guessed, with little buds of breasts just showing
through the blouse she wore and was already out-
growing.

I took the package from her and asked her name.
Alice Packer, she said. Kitty Packer was her aunt—her
grand-aunt, really. Kitty was the full-time librarian in
Nansquett now, and I knew the package contained the
few belongings Karen had not taken from the library
when she had driven off that rainy day. I took the parcel and smiled, and suddenly I realized what Alice
Packer was doing there on my property, where no one
else dared to come—she was somehow the link to my
future self, and without scaring or revolting her, I had
to impress her.

I asked if she were tired from her walk, or thirsty. She
hesitated, and I asked if she would like some milk or
cookies. She still hesitated. She'd heard enough with
her young ears about me and Chas and Karen to be
wary. Yet she was fascinated; I could see that outweigh-
ing her fears. Would she like to see the Pritchard man-

sion, I asked. It was an exact restoration of the way the house looked over a hundred years ago. No one from town had ever seen it. Alice would be the first. And I, the proprietor, would give her a special guided tour.

And it worked. Alice's older brother had done some of the carpentry work, she said, and had said that it was the most beautiful house he had ever seen. He'd talked so much about the place, that she'd wanted to have him take her to see it, she told me. So I knew the link to my future was a real one: How many children in Nansquett, in the entire state, would want to see a restored Victorian mansion?

And she was impressed. After the longish walk up to the house and the promised snack in the breakfast room, I guided her through the various rooms, watching her with as much intense interest as she showed in looking at the beds, the old furniture, the paintings, the curious decorations she'd never seen before. She was most taken with the collection of Amity's dolls, most of which I'd had restored at some cost by an old man in Coventry who specialized in nineteenth-century dolls. It was while she was gingerly handling one of the porcelain dolls that I realized how I could make a life-long impression on her: I decided to give her one of the dolls—the one she most admired, a rare and perfect object, played with by a little girl a hundred and fifteen years before, dressed like a pioneer woman in check-ered gingham, with a frilled mob cap and little patent leather shoes. Alice was so thrilled, but she refused the doll, and I had to insist on her taking it.

We shook hands once we reached Atwood Avenue again, as I had decided to walk her back out. She thanked me for her gift, clutched under one arm, and said she had had one of the loveliest afternoons of her life. She even reached up and planted a tiny kiss on my chin, saying she was going to tell everyone what a nice, polite man I was. Pretty Alice Packer, with a taste for the past: my link somehow to the future.

There is only one remaining task for me, now that I have established that link: I must prepare for the future so that it comes again—the triad, the situation, the three of us, the twist in the coil.

Amity understood that, understood after many readings and much speculation and deep thought that, with Constance and Eugene gone, her life had no meaning, that it had to be ended as soon as possible in order to set up the coil once more.

Will my future self come upon these journals of mine someday here in the Pritchard Museum and suddenly realize how we are all linked together? I have to believe that. That is why the house shall be a museum. I've already arranged that through my lawyer. A restored mansion from the nineteenth century, with a few contemporary amenities. The upkeep will be paid by the foundation I have established through my estate. A curator will be maintained by the county and the foundation. Yes, I'm certain that my future self—he or she, for the gender will make no difference at all—will come to this turreted library and lift this little red notebook, bound in morocco, and read it and come to recognize himself or herself and understand...

Understand why it was that on this date, I, Roger Lynch, aged thirty years old, of sound mind and body, threw myself into the newly repaired well and drowned until dead...

And will understand that he or she and I and Amity Pritchard are one.